Heishi

Shifting Planes Series: Book 1

Jeff Sabean

ISBN: 978-1-0868-5063-5

Dedication

First, I would like to thank my loving and patient wife Beckey, who has been there through this whole journey for me. My son Zane has been reading this story as I wrote it and has been my go-to guy for reading level difficulty. The rest of my children, Alyssa, Titus, Jade, and Mia have been ultra-supportive and have given me so many ideas for new ways to take my stories. Alyssa, my Cutie Pie, started me on this journey, as she was writing her own stories and reminded me how much I love to write. Thank you all for putting up with me as I obsessed over this, it never would have happened without all your support.

Next, I would be remiss to not thank my D&D group from my last trip to the desert. Torres, the pain in the neck GM, gave me the ideas behind some of the characters and such. Carty and Gonzo, you wild animals, for the relationship you two had in our game that helped me shape the characters I added to the book for you. Archer, for stepping up our game when you joined our party and taught us to think outside the box for in game combat and reminded us that rogues can in fact steal from their own party (just never from your healer!). I would like to thank Pritts for having an amazing moustache and bringing humor to every session. Kuster, who joined our campaign at the very end, but was one of the first to volunteer to read my first few chapters and give me feedback on them. And last but not least Applegate, who made fun of us relentlessly for months until you tried playing and found out how fun it was. Thank you all for allowing me to steal some ideas from our sessions to add as Easter eggs to bring some comedy to the book and for proof reading for me.

Lastly, I would like to thank J.T. Williams, author of the Half-Elf Chronicles (among many, many other books). If not for him, I would still be fumbling around on my own trying to figure out how to publish my story. He is a gentleman and was instrumental in getting me on the right path to make this dream happen.

Table of Contents

Prologue - The Call

Dawn. A beautiful time of the day filled with expectation and wonder as the sun breaks the horizon in a brilliant display of color. This morning seems more beautiful than normal, with a light haze still hanging around the base of the hill where the two combatants kneel facing each other. Their weapons are placed just to the sides of their legs, while they kneel just outside of each other's reach, as dictated by protocol. The peacefulness of the morning deceptively covers the promise of upcoming violence. Aki is inhumanly relaxed, with his eyes closed and his mind wandering as he takes in the sounds and smells of the hillside around him. A slight breeze blows through his hair that he keeps cropping shorter and shorter to hide the salt and pepper that is appearing around the edges. For a moment he lets his mind wander as he decides whether it is time to take it all off, or if he should embrace the "aged master" look. At 6'2" he has a height advantage over his opponent, but his greatest advantage is the decades he has spent mastering his arts. His tonfa, his choice of weapons for the day, are laying on the ground near his knees, one on each side of his legs. He is vigilantly aware of the movements of the younger man and smiles to himself at the thought of the upcoming battle. He will let this moment linger a while longer before beginning, as this is his favorite time of the day.

Heishi appears edgy; clearly nervous about being so close to the legendary master kneeling across from him. Although he has youth on his side, he isn't foolish enough to believe it will be all he needs to best the wizened warrior sitting opposite him. At 5'8" he realizes that Aki has a reach advantage, as do most men he squares off against, which might be one reason he gravitated to the long sword as his primary melee weapon. He moves with the practiced precision of a man who has performed this ritual of respect more times than he can possibly remember, but there remains a slight jerkiness to his actions that reveal an internal struggle to remain calm. As he closes his eyes to take a moment to focus before the combat begins, he can't help but be a little impressed that he has made it to this point. His katana lays peacefully near his left knee, and he is keenly aware of the swift death he can invoke at will when he wields the blade. His years of training and perseverance will hopefully pay off this morning, and then he will take his place in history as a master himself.

Aki gradually opens his eyes and gives a slight grunt to signal he is ready to proceed. Simultaneously, the two opponents bend at the waist and bow deeply, placing their foreheads to the ground in a sign of mutual respect. The bow is held for a few seconds, and slowly the men begin to return to their starting positions. Without warning, Heishi reaches down and grips the saya, or scabbard, for his blade in his left hand, lifts it and smoothly pulls the blade as he steps forward with his right foot. The jet-black blade arcs toward his opponent, light being absorbed by all but the ha, the cutting edge, which catches and reflects the light as it flashes with blinding speed. With a thought, he activates the blade and lightning flashes, leaving a green edged trail of electricity as the blade blazes toward Aki's forehead. From this distance it is impossible to get a killing blow, so the classic first strike is to aim for the forehead to hopefully make a clean cut and draining blood into your opponent's eyes. A fight typically would not begin until both opponents have completed the bow and returned to a standing position, but Heishi is depending on his slight breach of protocol to give him an edge in this fight.

The ploy almost succeeded, but this is not the first time an opponent has attempted subterfuge to defeat Aki. Just prior to the attack, the younger warrior made a fatal flaw and flinched before he reached for his blade, which was all the warning the veteran needed. As the blade flashes toward his face, Aki effortlessly reaches for the tonfa handles laying near his knees. Quickly and naturally, he raises his right hand with the handle gripped loosely. Just as the katana blade comes in range, Aki activates the weapon with a thought and shadows curl around the tonfa Aki designed himself. The blade stops inches from his face, the shadows absorb the impact and the lightning energy from the sword, and the old warrior smiles mercilessly.

"You'll pay for that, kid." Aki mutters as he uses the momentum of the swing to spin his opponent like a top. His left hand follows through with his second tonfa aimed for Heishi's midsection and would have crushed the ribs of a lesser man, but such would not be the case today. Heishi's first strike was a calculated risk, and although it did not pay off, he was not surprised and maintains his balance. He lightly rolls to the side as the second tonfa curves for his belly and deftly dodges the bludgeoning strike.

Disentangled from the initial encounter, both warriors now circle each other, watching for any flaw in his opponent's defense. Aki feints with his left, attempting to force Heishi to follow the movement, but knowing his enemy well the feint fails: *Aki favors his right, not his left.* While he is momentarily off balance from the feint, Heishi attempts a second cut swinging for

Aki's neck just above his left shoulder. Predictably, Aki moves to deflect the blow, but by the time his tonfa reaches the spot where the blade should be, Heishi has already pulled it back and is stabbing forward from his waist. Shocked, Aki reflexively jumps back and narrowly escapes disembowelment. As the two regain their footing, Heishi presses his attack with a swing straight down the center toward Aki's skull. A momentary look of terror crosses Aki's face as he realizes he might be late with his block, which causes overconfidence in his opponent. Rather than a slicing motion, he chops with the sword as if it is an axe, which slows the attack and affords the elder warrior the opportunity to deflect the blade with his left hand.

Pulling down and to the right with all the strength he can muster, Aki is able to step out of the kill zone and pull his opponent off balance. Spinning behind Heishi, he attempts to finish this duel quickly but is too slow: his tonfa meets nothing but air where his target was a fraction of a second before. Surprised, he misses his block as the katana comes straight for his head again, sparks crackling as if the blade itself is excited to spill his blood. At the last second, Heishi pulls the swing short and only slices an eighth of an inch into the right side of Aki's temple, leaving a five-inch-long gash across his head. As the blade slices through flesh, the electricity arcing across the blade cauterizes the wound, leaving no blood but creating a wicked looking scar in the process. As Aki prepares a counterattack to draw some blood of his own, both men are stopped suddenly by a loud, high pitched alarm coming from Heishi's wrist communicator, signaling an encrypted message inbound. They each take a step away from each other, not yet dropping their guard.

With a grin, Heishi lowers his blade and deactivates the electricity pulsing through it. He bows from the waist to his opponent, and Aki follows suit as his wrist communicator begins emitting an identical alarm.

"Next time you won't be saved by the bell, old man," laughs Heishi as he returns his blade to its saya and checks the message.

"You still have much to learn kid," smiles Aki, "but I clearly have taught you well."

As the message decrypts, Heishi's grin widens. "Meet you in the team room in an hour," he says as he mounts his Harley and begins receiving acknowledgements from the rest of his team. "It's time to make the green grass grow."

Chapter One - The Jump

Ninety minutes later, Heishi, also known as Master Sergeant Paul Neasba, Team Leader of an elite Special Operations unit code named "Ronin," sat reviewing the mission notes as his team streaked away from Fort Bragg on their C-17. His team had been activated in response to a nuclear threat in Florida, and due to the nature of the emergency the team hadn't had time for a briefing: just pack your junk and get on the bird. The flight would take under three hours, but the team had been together long enough that they could operate with minimal instruction, and three hours was plenty of time to work out the details.

Looking down the plane at his team prepping their gear, MSG Neasba couldn't help but feel a sense of pride in what he had put together over the past 18 months. It all began with a directive from the President to develop a Top-Secret team of operatives who would be ready to deploy immediately, bypassing the typical Washington D. C. bureaucracy. The Special Operations community had learned their lesson from the implementation of Delta Force:

once the public learned of your existence, your ability to operate without red tape was greatly diminished. Ronin Team could technically be considered illegal if the wrong people went snooping, which explained the secrecy surrounding the team. They were funded by several third-party sources that could never be traced back to the US Government, the Tactical Operations Center (TOC) was in a subterranean bunker beneath an artillery impact zone, everyone associated with the team had falsified identities, and only a select few high-ranking officials even knew of their existence. Their mission was to perform the jobs that no one else could, and to leave no evidence they were ever there.

Chief Warrant Officer Adam Zatus was quiet, but none of the tech used by the team would exist without his brilliance, to include the weapons used in the morning sparring session between Heishi and Aki. He had always possessed the ability to break down components and re-arrange them to maximize their power while reducing the weight, which was crucial for operatives in the field. It did no good to have the coolest tech in the history of the world if you needed a four-man team to carry it to the destination. CW3 Zatus was responsible for the gadgets that were sold to the public to partially fund Ronin Team, but he withheld the best tech for the team and kept it classified so the enemy would never know what was coming their way. Would a wrist-mounted, nuclear powered, encrypted communicator that had no need of satellites, provided videoconference capabilities, automatically translated any spoken language, and didn't need to be charged for an estimated 200 years be useful in the private sector? Of course, it would. But the minute the technology was released to the public, the enemy would know about it and attempt to hack it. Some things were best kept secret.

Aki, also known as Sergeant First Class Jay Aki, the team medic, was busy re-packing his gear to include some of Zatus' latest tech. Having served on Special Forces teams for longer than anyone had the nerve to discuss with him, Aki had spent his entire adult life keeping Soldiers alive. Over the past few years, this had become much easier, not to mention his ruck getting lighter, thanks to the new tech available. The medical advances made by CW3 Zatus' tech had saved thousands of lives worldwide, and combat deaths were down proportionately. A running joke on the team was that if Zatus made saving lives any easier, Aki would be out of a job. One can dream, right?

In the rear of the plane, blasting old school rock n roll while reconfiguring his gear, was the final member of the tactical team, Staff Sergeant Tyler Tiane. SSG Tiane was the team's youngest member as well as the sniper, and was being groomed by MSG Neasba to eventually take over as the team lead because let's be honest, gun fighters need to know when to take a desk job if they want to live to be an old gun fighter. Specializing in guerrilla tactics and improvisation on the battlefield, Tiane possessed a rare ability to look at a situation from a "bird's eye view" and make brilliant, although often extremely dangerous, decisions on the spot. Neasba reminded himself as he looked at Tiane that with experience the cocky young man would gain wisdom to go with his knowledge, and when that happened the world would be a much safer place.

"Finish what you're doing and get up here for a mission brief," called MSG Neasba, "We have about 2 hours before we jump, and there is a lot of information to cover in that time."

Tiane, always eager to please his team leader, was the first to the briefing table. "What's the mission, boss?" He asked as the other two slid into their seats.

Looking at his team, Neasba was filled with pride at what he had put together. Knowing his next bit of information was volatile, he waited for his team's undivided attention before continuing.

"Listen up Ronin Team," Neasba began, "I hate to do this as we are about to enter a hostile situation, but it was sprung on me after the bird was in the air. We been doing such great things for our country that the boss in the White House has decided to expand our little dysfunctional family. Please welcome our new intelligence officer, Captain Leigh Aldith. Yes, CPT Aldith understands that you are still my team and she is simply the Intelligence Advisor, so there will be no power struggles around here. My word is still undisputed, and she understands this. CPT Aldith comes highly recommended, and I am assured she will fit in with our team. Unfortunately, we do not have time for bonding now, so leave the usual shenanigans for after the mission and pretend to be professionals for the next couple hours. CPT Aldith, the floor is yours."

Stepping around the corner, all eyes were immediately drawn to the remarkable woman standing before them. Dressed in yoga pants, tennis shoes, a loose t-shirt, and a wide-brimmed hat, CPT Aldith appeared to be dressed to visit a theme park for the day, not to brief a Special Operations team. All she was missing was a fanny pack to complete her tourist ensemble. Standing 5'6" and weighing 145 lbs. With blonde hair and blue eyes, she appeared to be physically fit, and the smirk on her face belied her readiness to shut down any smart comments that might be forthcoming. Fortunately, Ronin Team were professionals, and would not allow their typical hazing rituals to interfere with a mission. Following a short round of introductions, the briefing commenced.

"We have rock solid intel that terrorists have smuggled a nuclear weapon into the United States across the Mexican border and the latest information has it located within the new theme park in Orlando, where it hasn't moved for at least 48 hours. Zatus' email sniffer picked up a trail through fake Gmail accounts that appear to be legitimate threats against the Christmas celebration: this might come as a surprise, but religious extremists seem to have a problem with a celebration that can be traced back to a different religion. We have less than four hours until the parade begins, so that doesn't give us much time to get moving on this. We will be jumping into the outskirts of the park where local security will provide us transportation. We'll be operating within the park, so civilian clothes are the uniform, and all weapons must be hidden. If you can make it look like a costume for the park, then bring it, but I don't want to see any of your faces on the news tonight. Keep it low profile, conceal your pistols, this one will be difficult to keep out of the media, but try anyway. Questions?"

"Did you say 'we' ma'am?" asked Neasba while trying to contain the shocked look on his face.

"Affirmative, Master Sergeant, I will be accompanying the team for the jump. Before you get defensive, allow me to explain. First, I will not be involved in the operational aspect of the mission. I would never endanger your team by changing the team dynamics at the last minute. My sole purpose will be to secure a position with park security so I can feed real time information to you. With more prep time, I understand that CW3 Zatus could provide me that information without leaving the bird, but we don't have that kind of time today. By accompanying the team to the ground, Zatus will stay with you and have more time to set up without having to worry about providing a feed to me.

"Second, if needed, I will assist you with blending in with park visitors. Females are not exactly common among Special Operations, so if the enemy is looking for a group of guys with short hair who are gunning for them, you will stand out like a sore thumb. Add a woman into the mix, especially against an enemy who considers females as subservient to males, and I will help you move more easily through the park. I already acknowledged that this is still your team, and I take all commands on ground from you, Master Sergeant, but this is not a negotiation."

As the rest of the team stifled amused grins, MSG Neasba stared at CPT Aldith without blinking for a full ten seconds before nodding his head and breaking into a smile.

"Fair enough, ma'am, how should we address you in public?"

"Leigh is fine, unless you want to pose as my husband and come up with some kind of inappropriate pet name to call me in public?" replied CPT Aldith.

"It would appear you'll fit right in, Sugar Butt," laughed Neasba as he ducked a coffee mug she tossed at his head. "Now, if we can get back to business, we need the data on the DZ (drop zone), background information on the park security we will link up with, and any information we have on this terrorist organization. While you brief us, the team will change into civilian camouflage..."

An hour and a half later, the team was beginning to feel like the dead horse had been beaten enough. Zatus had taken control of an NSA satellite to provide a real time feed of the park, which had then been scrutinized from every possible angle. Ronin Team felt like they knew every hole and rock in the DZ, park security was already milling in the area and keeping park goers' attention elsewhere, all comms had been tested, parachutes were rigged, and the team was waiting semi-patiently for the green light. As far as they knew, no one had ever jumped into a theme park before, but unfortunately no one would ever know about this Op, so there would be no way to brag about this later. Oh, well, these guys didn't do it for bragging rights, they did it to keep people safe.

Neasba went down the line performing his Pre-Combat Checks. He had pulled up the park's website and sent a request to park security to have a costume standing by on the DZ. This would allow him to hide his pistols and carry his sword around as part of the costume. He chuckled at his good luck: one of the park's characters was an anime Samurai Warrior in full medieval armor. He reached back and ensured his sword was fastened in his weapon's case on his leg: if his black hats knew he would be rigging up a katana in his weapons case instead of an M4 they would have never believed it. The little ironies in life were fun. Neasba moved to Aki to check his gear. A costume would be waiting at the DZ for Aki as well, and one suited for him: the ninja villain from the Samurai cartoon. This could very well be one of the team's more interesting missions. He wondered for a minute if they would get to ride that new roller coaster before they were extracted. First thing first, got to stop a nuclear explosion...you know, the minor details.

Moving on to Zatus, he was impressed once again with the Chief's equipment loadout. Neasba remembered the "good old days" when his Communication Sergeant would carry at least a hundred pounds of gear, but Zatus appeared to be carrying less than the rest of the team. That worked out well considering he was going to have to blend into the crowd in civilian clothes alongside Aldith. His tablet device was secure, and the Chief could do more with that tablet than most nerds could do with a full-sized computer. He was going to need all his expertise today, because they had a very small window before terrorists made Florida glow at night.

As he stopped to check Tiane, he realized that the young Staff Sergeant had broken down his sniper rifle and stored it in a tourist-looking backpack that he had rigged below his reserve parachute hanging from his chest. Smart. The team would be in good hands if Tiane could get to the top of the "mountain" roller coaster in the center of the park without drawing suspicion. From there he could reach out and touch every corner of the park: all the team would need to do was stay within sight of the "mountain" and they would have the best shooter in the world covering them. Of course, Tiane looked like a little punk in civilian clothes. No one is perfect.

Last in line was his wild card: CPT Aldith. She was in the same clothes, but now she had a parachute rigged up and a communicator strapped to her wrist compliments of Zatus. Neasba had to assume she was hiding weapons somewhere, but the yoga pants made it hard to imagine where they might be. Fortunately, the Master Sergeant had been in the Army long enough to know better than to ask. All he needed to do was ensure her parachute was rigged properly so she would survive the jump. It would be frowned upon to let her die on her first mission. Maybe next time.

"One Minute!"

The C-17 Crew Chief opens the tailgate.

Adrenaline pumping. Neasba makes eye contact with each member of the team: you would have to shake his guys to know they were awake, but CPT Aldith clearly is trying to hold her emotions in check.

The first time is always the hardest, but she'll be fine if she remembers to pull her chute.

"Thirty Seconds!"

GREEN LIGHT

Neasba gave the team the thumbs up and lem off the tailgate of the plane at 25,000 feet. This was a HALO jump: High Altitude, Low Opening. The team did not want anyone to see them coming and panic, and there was no time to land and fight traffic getting onto the park property. All five members of Ronin Team cleared the rear of the aircraft and began the freefall to the park.

At 8,000 feet, there was a bright flash and clouds surrounded the team out of nowhere. At first it seemed like a blessing to help mask their descent, but then the lightning started. At terminal velocity there is not much reason to be paranoid, as they would be through the clouds and ready to pull in less than 30 seconds, but then the lightning turned blood red. Checking his altimeter, MSG Neasba got scared for the first time since his very first static line jump at Fort Benning when he was 18 years old: rather than dropping in elevation, he was rising again!

Paranoid, he broke comm silence and ordered the team to check in with their altitude reading:

"Ronin Two: 9,000 feet and....rising? Top, what is going on here?" Zatus all but shouted into the communicator.

"Keep it down, 2. What do you have 3?"

"Ronin Three: 9,500 feet and rising...that can't be right, can it Top?" Aki chimed in.

"Ronin Four: 10,000 feet and holding steady, boss. Seriously? Is anyone else showing we're not moving at all?" Tiane was starting to let the panic show in his voice.

"Ronin Five: 10,000 feet and not moving, Master Sergeant." Aldith somehow was now keeping her cool better than the rest of the team. The wind was still whipping around the team, just like it should be, but the dropping sensation had ceased. The feeling was like being in a parachute simulator, which the team did out on Raeford Road with a date sometimes just for fun. It was not what should be happening now, as the blood red lightning continued to crackle around them, and the wind began to swirl counterclockwise.

"There's no way we jumped into a tornado, is there Top?" Tiane asked, clearly more shaken than the last time he spoke almost a full minute prior. "I mean, have you ever even HEARD of any crazy nonsense like this?"

Silence reigned on the radio for another full minute before anyone else spoke.

"Ronin Two, do you have any clue what is going on here? You are the expert on weird things, did one of your toys break and do this to us?" Neasba's voice did not give away a single bit of the paranoia that was now sneaking into his brain as he floated there in mid-air, 10,000 feet above the ground.

No answer.

"Zatus, seriously, if you don't answer me, I am gonna throat punch you if I can ever reach you again. Do you have any idea what is going on here?"

"Top, I don't think he's conscious. I can see his chest moving, so he's breathing, but I can't see his eyes." Aki responded. "He still has his oxygen mask on, which is a good thing, but it's keeping me from seeing his eyes."

"Four, can you see his eyes? Can you see if he is moving at all?" Neasba asked, the concern creeping into the edges of his voice. It was one thing to be stuck in mid-air, it was another for his tech genius to be unconscious for no reason while he was trying to find a way to get down.

Lightning cracked again, closer this time. "I can't see his face at all, Top, from the waist up all I see is cloud now," Tiane responded.

Neasba switched to the Command channel. "TOC, this is Ronin One. I'm sure you are imagining the equipment is malfunctioning on your end right now, but we truly did ascend back to 10,000 feet and are holding steady here in the middle of an electrical storm. With red lightning. And the wind is circling backwards. Ronin Two is also unconscious and unresponsive but appears to be breathing. So, what do you see on YOUR end?"

"Ronin One, this is Ronin Six. Say again last, over." The radio operator in the TOC sounded almost as puzzled as Neasba felt.

"Six, this is One, you heard me alright, we

dropped to 8,000 feet, then ascended back to 10,000 feet, and are hanging out here in mid-air staring at each other. All except for Zatus, who appears to be unconscious but breathing, which is pissing me off because if one of his toys malfunctioned and did this, I may just kill him later. I really would love to hear what you are seeing from the bird, over."

The team waited as patiently as possible for a response from the TOC, but there was silence on the net. Dead silence. Silence so loud it was hard to hear. Even the noise from the wind died, as the team hung in midair completely motionless.

Without warning, the team was falling again at a rapid rate. Neasba looked over to Zatus to try to control his descent and saw something that was impossible: his eyes were glowing with a silver light.

Great, thought Neasba, now I've completely lost my mind. I guess there's no going back now...

Looking at his altimeter, his surprise was complete as he saw it spinning out of control in his descent. As he was about to lose what was left of his sanity, the clouds broke, and he saw the ground rushing up at him close enough that he could see the trees on the top of the roller coaster mountain.

"Ronin team pull your chutes NOW! Pull

Pull Pull!!!" Neasba screamed into his radio.

As his parachute deployed, Neasba had just enough time to count three other parachutes before there was a flash of red and his world went black.

Chapter 2 - The World

Neasba woke up at the base of a mountain with his parachute still attached and intermittently filling and deflating in the wind. Looking around, he realized he had been dragged for over thirty feet after he hit the ground, so he released the straps of his harness and wiggled out of it before any more damage could be done. The sky was dark, and no stars were visible, so he was having difficulty determining the time of day.

How long was I out? Where is the rest of my team? And what in the world was that freak storm? The weather report was for clear skies, and that storm was crazy, even for Florida…

Cautiously getting to his feet, he took stock of his situation: no broken bones, just some bruises, and all his gear seemed to be undamaged. As he ran his hand around his head, he felt a small patch of dried blood on the left side toward the back.

Well, if it's dry then it can't be too bad, right?

He pulled his chute to himself and looked for a place to conceal it.

Hmm…I don't remember there being so many in the park, and why are there no lights?

As he looked around the area, his memory started to clear. There was a flash before the clouds and lightning. Did the bomb explode? That couldn't be it, otherwise there would be nothing left. The mountain in front of him looked like an actual mountain, not part of an amusement park ride. In fact, it appeared to be larger than the whole park should have been. What could possibly be going on around here?

"Any Ronin element, this is Ronin One, come in." MSG Neasba realized he was holding his breath as he waited for an answer.

Nothing.

He tried a dozen more times, and finally decided there was something wrong with his communication equipment. No worries, he knew how to operate independently until he could contact his element. But the bigger problem remained: where was he, and which direction should he go? Based on the satellite feed, he needed to head East to get to the park security office, but he wasn't sure where he landed, or if he was even in the park. Could he have been blown that far off course? There were no REAL mountains in Florida, so that should narrow it down, but that was clearly a mountain in front of him.

After burying his parachute as a good Paratrooper should, Neasba decided to arbitrarily pick a direction and begin walking. Naturally he didn't have a compass since he was supposed to parachute into a theme park, and none of his electronics were giving accurate directions, so he decided to use the only method he knew to navigate a maze: always turn right. Looking to his right, he picked a path that skirted the trees and lead into an open area of relatively even ground. Keeping the mountain on his left side, he headed off, keeping vigilant for potential enemies while also listening for running water or anything else that would lead him to some type of civilization.

Several hours later, a glow appeared above the trees in the distance to his half left. Picking up the pace a bit, he forgot to maintain his vigilance. From tree line to his left, he heard a faint growl that tipped him off to the danger. He turned toward the sound a split second before a dark form skimmed over his head, landing to his right. As he turned toward the dark shape, he saw what appeared to be a rat the size of a bear skidding around to face him, it's eyes glowing yellow in the faint light coming through the gloom. Halfway through its turn, the giant rat clearly realized it lost the element of surprise and stood up from all four legs to two. Neasba tried to control his shock as he dove to the side, narrowly avoiding the jaws of the beast that snapped closed where his head had been a moment before.

Having recovered from his initial shock, Neasba decided to use his katana to defend himself from this beast: having no idea where he was, a pistol could bring unwanted attention to himself. Keeping his eyes on the rat monster, he swiftly slid his blade from its saya on his back and put its razor-sharp blade between himself and the beast. A spark of recognition flashed in the eyes of the beast as the dim light glinted off the edge blade, but still it came on with blinding speed. A claw came in from his left side, which Neasba blocked with the mune, the back of his blade, which kept the cutting edge facing his enemy. With a thought he ignited the lightning properties of his blade and slid it cleanly through the giant rat, cutting it cleanly from its left hip to its right shoulder. As the monster fell apart and the two halves dropped to the ground, the beast, still unaware that it was already dead, filled the air with a scream that echoed across the field. Neasba watched as the beast completed its death throes, deactivated the lightning, cleaned his blade, and replaced it in its saya.

The entire fight lasted less than ten

seconds, but in that time his world had changed. What was that beast? Where had it come from? And the ever-nagging question Neasba had been asking since he awakened in this strange place: where was he? Shrugging off the questions, he continued toward the light in the distance, hoping he would find answers when he reached civilization.

An hour later, the field ran across a path of hard packed dirt. Upon inspection, Neasba decided that it was used regularly, and what appeared to be wagon wheel ruts were visible along the edges of the path. It was hardly the strangest thing he had witnessed in the past three hours, but worth making a mental note of. Not wanting to be out in the dark in this place any longer than he needed to be, he took a couple steps off the road and cautiously began following it in the direction of the lights he saw coming through the trees.

The sun was creeping over the hills behind him as he came around the last turn and got a view of the source of the light. If the giant rat had surprised him, the sight before him rocked him back on his heels completely. He was looking down on what appeared to be a town inside of a roughly pentagon shaped stone wall with towers at each of the corners. From what he could see over the wall, it appeared the buildings inside were mostly constructed of wood and reminded him of the medieval faire he had attended as a child. Smoke trickled out of the few chimneys he could see dotting the town, and a cart was rolling down one of the dirt roads visible from his vantage point. Through the light fog and thickening chimney smoke, he could just see the glint of the morning sun reflecting off a body of water.

This looks like a port of some sort. That can't be right. There isn't anywhere like this left in the world. How hard did I hit my head on that landing?

Keeping an eye on the road behind him, Neasba stepped onto the side and headed down to the town. The closer he came to the town; he began to realize the wall was taller than it at first appeared. He estimated the front wall to be approximately a mile long and stood twenty feet high. Approaching the gate, a smaller door became noticeable set into the wall beside the larger gate. Assuming this was for foot traffic, he tentatively approached and knocked on the door. A barred window appeared in front of him, and a light shined through the portal into his face, blinding him as to the speaker on the other side.

"What do you want? I'm sitting down to break my fast and you are interrupting!" A deep voice sounded through the window. The speaker clearly was used to being in control of his gate, and his impatience was coming through loud and clear.

Neasba hadn't even thought of what he would say when he got to the gate, so he stumbled for a second and stared dumbly at the light.

Ok, don't give away too much information. If I tell him about the rat monster, he's likely to slam the door in my face or put me in the looney bin.

Deciding on the spot to not give away even his alias, Neasba unconsciously slipped into the nickname given to him by his team:

"I'm Heishi. I got separated from my, uh, group, a way back in the dark. I'm not sure where I am, but if you could let me in so I can get some food and a place to sleep for a while I would appreciate it."

After a moment of silence from the other side in which he could feel eyes scrutinizing him, Heishi heard a disgusted grunt as the window slammed closed. As he debated knocking again or walking away, he heard a bar slide through a latch, and the door swung back just far enough for him to slip through. As his eyes adjusted to the light, he realized he was standing inside a mantrap: the wall was apparently thicker than he had estimated, as he was standing in a room approximately five feet wide and ten feet deep, with a fireplace set into the wall on his right. The source of the light was a blazing fire that kept the room glowing in surreal light, although the temperature seemed to remain comfortable.

His surprise was complete when the door slammed shut and he found himself staring at the strangest man he had ever laid eyes on. Standing slightly over six feet tall, the guard was not the most imposing person in the world: except for his green skin. His unkempt black hair fell across the side of his face to his shoulders and peeking out from uneven bangs his eyes glowed red in the light from the fire. A scowl was clear on his face, and the tusks protruding from his lower jaw moved back and forth threateningly as he ground his teeth staring at Heishi. The guard was clearly dressed to fight in close quarters should a threat present itself: he was clad in leather armor that would not stand up on a battlefield of this era but would protect him in a room where swinging a sword would be limited. He wore no other gear that could encumber him at this range, but at his sides were what would be classified somewhere between a large dagger and a short sword with wicked-looking serrations on both edges of the blades. His hands hung loosely near the hilts of his blades, clearly ready and proficient at putting them to work in the blink of an eye.

"Where are you coming from? Who are you? Keep your hands where I can see them, human, or I'll cut you to pieces and feed you to the dogs."

Great, way to hit it off with the monster-man. I guess it's a good thing I didn't mention the rat monster, he probably wouldn't have been impressed. For all I know, he might kill me for not letting it eat me.

Slouching a bit to try to look less imposing, Heishi took on the role of a subservient medieval peasant, and started into what he hoped was a reasonable request:

"Honorable guard, as I stated, I lost my group out in the wilderness on the other side of that mountain. I followed the light from this city from a distance, and after walking all night I just reached your gate. I am hungry and tired and would like nothing more than a hot meal and a room if you could direct me to the closest inn."

The guard looked contemptuously at Heishi and growled a bit. "Hey, human, don't think because I have a bit of orc blood in me that I'm stupid. I recognize a fighter when I see one, so stop playing me for a fool." His hands twitched as he eased them across to rest on the hilts of his blades. "Not only did I watch you slinking down the road like an assassin, but you have blood that clearly is not your own on your arm. Want to try your explanation again?"

Heishi stepped back a pace and blinked when the guard said, "orc blood," but other than that he thought he did a good job of keeping his poker face. Slowly, he lifted his hands in front of him to keep them clear of any weapons he had on his body and looked the orc-man in the face.

"Good guard, I gave my name, but have not gotten yours in turn. May I ask your name so I can properly address you?" Heishi was in control of his emotions and thinking clearly for the first time since stepping through the door.

The guard stiffened a bit, straightening up to his full height, and his scowl deepened. "You may call me guard and answer my questions quickly or you will leave this room in pieces."

Drawing on his memory of medieval times, Heishi decided to play the role of the honorable knight. "Very well, Guard. I was traveling as a guard for four companions, three male and one female. We were attacked by giant rats in the darkness and separated, and I was unable to locate them. In the distance I saw the light from your city and made my way this direction hoping they would do the same. I would appreciate if you would tell me if they have come by here and point me to an inn where I can get a meal and a place to sleep."

Guard eased a bit at the honest answer and appeared pensive. "You have a strange dialect, and your garb is not from a region I recognize. Where do you come from, Heishi?"

Deciding honestly would either get him

arrested as a lunatic or straighten out the mess he was in, Heishi decided either way he should get a meal out of it. "I come from a planet called Earth, in a country called the United States of America. I was with my companions when a storm erupted around us, I was lifted into the sky while red lightning flashed around us, and then hurtled toward the ground again. I was knocked unconscious and woke up on the other side of that mountain, separated from my companions. I do not know where I am or how I got here, and I apologize for not being forthright with the information, but I did not want you to think me a lunatic. If there is someone who can help me, I am in dire need."

The longer he spoke, the more he realized Guard was leaning closer and closer with every word, and when he finished there was a long pause before Guard snapped back to a standing position. A grin split his face, and he slapped Heishi on the shoulder.

"There now, human, that was not so hard, was it? I have heard stories of this red lightning and shifts between the planes of existence, although I am not well versed in such matters. I assume you also have no gold for a room or meal?"

Heishi blanched at the question. "Honestly I had not thought of currency yet. I was more concerned with finding civilization, and to be truthful was surprised at your appearance, as orcs are legends in my, uh, plane of existence. Is there a place I may work to earn a meal and a place to sleep?"

Fully relaxed, Guard let out a belly laugh when he heard orcs described as a legend. "Yes, human, if you follow the main road straight to the docks, turn left and you will see an inn named 'The Portal.' Tell the bartender Shenroc sent you and that you are willing to work for a meal and a place to sleep. The Portal is not the safest place in the city, but it is the best place for you to find work. If you know how to use that blade you have slung on your back, it should be easy."

"Shenroc, it is a pleasure to meet you, and thank you," Heishi smiled.

"It is my pleasure, human. You may find answers to how you came here if you find the right person, just be polite, The Portal is not the place to start problems." Shenroc turned and lead Heishi to the door that lead to the city.

"Welcome to Terminus, Human."

Chapter 3 - The Portal

As Heishi walked through the door, he had to stop to adjust his bearings. The early morning light was dull compared to the raging fire light in the gate's mantrap, and as his eyes adjusted, he needed a moment to orient himself. Looking down what Shenroc referred to as the main road, Heishi felt like he had been transported back in time. Shops were opening along the stone road and vendors dragged carts into position along the way to set up for the day. The biggest shock, however, was the mixture of different races thought to be fantasy in his world. There were gnomes, dwarves, and orcs; there were humans as well, and occasionally he saw taller humans with pointed ears he assumed were real life elves.

Great. Everything I thought about the real world either changed overnight, or I'm suffering from a severe concussion. I had better get it together fast, because if this is real, I could be in serious trouble.

Slowly, Heishi started down the street, looking as closely as he dared at the assorted characters around him. The vendors whose carts were already set up watched him as well, and when he was within range began each began his or her sales pitch.

"Roasted rat, sir?"

"Ehh, you look like you could use some ale!"

"Ye can't be walkin' around without armor to protect ye!" A dwarf shouted as he passed what could only be a blacksmith shop. "Get in 'ere man, afore ye get killed to death out there!"

Smiling, Heishi shook his head in response, and decided he should pick up the pace before he got mobbed.

If they only knew I had no gold.

He followed the road for several miles and concluded that this main road was the marketplace for the city. The entire length was lined with vendors and shopkeepers, each looking to sell his wares. When the road dead ended into the docks, he turned left and saw a three-story building: the first floor was constructed stone, but the second and third stories were built of wood. From the walkways that lead around the second and third floors that reminded him of an old saloon and hotel from a western movie, he assumed he had found the right place.

As he turned toward the building, he narrowly avoided bumping into a warrior who was haggling with a road-side vendor. The woman was selling roasted rats, and apparently thought she was being cheated. "Guards! Thief! Thief!"

The warrior straightened to his full height, around seven feet tall, and put his hands up in a non-threatening manner. Heishi realized this warrior appeared to be a dwarf by all his features except his height. He had dark red hair that hung in a single braid that came to the center of his back, and a beard braided into three thick braids that hung to his belt. His baritone voice came across as smooth as silk, not with a typical Dwarvish brogue, as he looked down on the hag and said, "The only thing I am trying to steal is your heart."

The hag straightened her scraggly hair and parted it from her face, batted her eyelids at the hulking warrior, licked her chapped lips, and smiled, showing her single, rotting front tooth.

I need to move along before I get caught in something weird here...

Heishi carefully approached the front door, where the wooden sign hanging above his head was smashed in places but the words "The Portal" were readable in black paint. Walking through the front door, his senses were accosted with the smells of stale beer, smoke, and most of all fish. There was a haze that seemed to hang around the interior of the bar, although he couldn't see the source from where he was standing. Along the wall to his right was a row of booths, and there were about a dozen tables in the center of the room in no discernable order. The back of the room was taken up by a bar, and a rickety-looking staircase in the left rear of the room lead to the next level of the establishment. At this time of the morning the place was mostly empty, but there were several drunk patrons at the bar and at tables scattered around the room.

Cautiously, he slipped through the room, trying to keep at least a table or two between himself and the closest patrons: no need to risk offending a drunken patron when he had finally found a place to eat. Approaching the bar, he took a seat on a stool and waited patiently for the bartender to notice him. The bartender approached, and he was one of the most interesting characters Heishi had come across in all his travels...on both planes of existence. Standing about five feet tall, he could have passed for a dwarf, but he was not as solidly built as the other dwarfs he had encountered along the road: in fact, he was so skinny Heishi thought he might have to run around in the shower to get wet. He wore leggings for pants, which accentuated his scrawny legs and knobby knees, and he wore a sleeveless shirt and a vest. The little man had scraggly hair sticking out at different lengths and in just about every direction, but he was clean shaven. Knowing enough lore about dwarves, he knew no respectable dwarf would be seen without a beard. As he looked the bartender in the face, he realized the man had a glass eye, and that it was rolling around different directions as he looked at Heishi inquiringly.

"Eeehhhh, what can I get ya?" the man almost squeaked as he spoke.

"I would like a meal and something to drink, what do you have?" asked Heishi.

"Eeeehhhhhh, I have beer, and I have beer, or you can have beer, whaddayawant?" the little bartender giggled to himself.

Noticing that the bartender's eyes were rolling different directions, Heishi wondered if either of them, both, or even neither were made of glass. Shaking the thought from his head, he remembered he had no gold.

"Good sir, I ran into some problems on the road, and I have no gold. Shenroc at the gate told me that I would be able to find work here to pay for a meal and a place to rest?"

"Eeeeehhhhh, that Shenroc, always sending us work. Good man, good man," the bartender said. He then muttered something unintelligible under his breath, shifted his head the other direction, appeared to answer himself, shifted the other way and appeared to answer again, then giggled uncontrollably before turning back to Heishi. "You a fighter, human?"

"That depends on who you want me to kill," answered Heishi without blinking.

"HAHAHAHA, you humans, always wanting to kill someone! No no no no no, can you fight with no weapons? For money? No weapons, no weapons, and no one gets killed, just the first one to stop fighting loses," the bartender laughed as his left eye appeared to focus on Heishi and the other rolled the other way.

"Aye, I can fight," replied Heishi with a grin. "I am also looking for information about planes of existence, if you could point me toward someone who knows of such things."

"Eeeeeeehhhh, that kind of information isn't cheap, human. The Illustrious will let me give you beer, food, and a room until tonight, but you will have to fight to pay for it. Eeehhh, whassat? No, I didn't tell him yet. Eeehh, ok, yeah, uh huh, HAHAHAHA," the little guy seemed to get lost in a conversation with himself.

"Excuse me, kind sir, you were about to get me a beer and some food before showing me to a room," Heishi pointed the excitable bartender back in the right direction.

"Eeeeehhhh, yep yep yep, beer and food, beer and food," the bartender said to himself as he looked around, picked up a mug, and reached for the beer tap. He missed the tap, reached again, set the mug down, reached with both hands until he grasped the tap handle, then poured the beer. He slid a key across the bar to Heishi with the mug of beer, "Room 6, up one, no two, no one set of stairs, and find the number on the door. The Illustrious will expect you here when it gets dark to fight to pay for your room. Eeeehhh, what? Oh yeah, I'll get you some squid soup and bread, best in town. HAHAHA. Nah, best you can afford though, human!"

The room turned out to be on the third floor and was sparsely outfitted with a small bed with a straw mattress, a single chair, and a small table. He slid the chair over to the door and propped it under the handle to keep it shut. The door had a lock, but how many keys were there? Best not to take any chances. A window opened facing the water, and the smell of salt air drifted through, bringing back memories of vacations by the ocean.

Can't think about that now. I have a room, but I must keep my mind clear here. Maybe if I sleep, I will wake up and realize this is a bad dream. Or maybe this is reality and thoughts of home will just get me killed. Either way, I need to stay sharp...

After looking over every inch of the walls and convincing himself there would be no unwelcomed visitors, he slumped onto the bed. It was surprisingly clean, considering the condition of the rest of the place, and relatively comfortable. As his mind drifted back to memories of vacations at the beach, his exhaustion won, and he slipped into a fitful sleep.

Chapter 4 - The Boss

Dreams of the jump, of lifting in the air and floating amid flashes of red lightning permeated his sleep. He was falling, watching his teammates streaking for the ground. Then saw that silver light shining from Zatus' eyes. Was that a clue, or was he dreaming? If he was dreaming, would he know it? Had he even woken up at all? A scream escaped his lips as he jumped up, pulling his pistol from the holster on his thigh.

Still in this room. Still in this reality. I guess sleeping didn't help.

A bang on his door interrupted his thoughts, and a deep voice came through: "Hey, human, time to earn your room and board. Hurry up, boss don't like waiting."

Heishi rolled out of the bed, feeling like someone had beaten him with a bag of bricks. He cracked his neck, slung his sword on his back, and opened the door. Standing in front of him was what appeared to be a man whose muscles had muscles. He stood a few inches taller than Heishi's 5'8", and his skin glinted with a blue-grey tint. He was shirtless and carried a wicked looking sword with a blade serrated on both edges at his hip, and a strap across his chest appeared to hold a shield on his back. His face set Heishi back a bit, as the "man" had the face of a shark, with rows of razor-sharp teeth that protruded from his mouth through the grin that spread across his face as the door opened. His jet black, beady eyes bored into Heishi's jade orbs.

"Come on, human, you's can leave your weapons in the room, no one will steal in the boss's place. House rules, no shirt, no shoes, no weapons for fighters. Hurry up, boss don't like waiting," the shark man repeated.

"What do I call you?" Heishi asked he stripped down to the prescribed uniform for the fight.

"I's be the one who'll eat you if you's don't fight good for the boss," the shark man stated.

"Fair enough. Lead on, Hungry," Heishi quipped.

As the pair descended the stairs into the bar, Heishi noted the tables had all been moved to the edges of the room, and a ring of drunk patrons were watching two combatants slug it out in the middle. Beer was flowing, the smoke was thick, and the crowd particularly raucous as one clearly won the battle.

"You's up, funny guy. Fight good or the

boss says I kin eat you," the shark man said as he shoved Heishi into the circle of customers.

Great, I was hoping to see a fight first. I didn't even see how the last guy won.

The blood stains on the floor spoke for themselves as to how brutal the fights could be.

I'll just have to win fast.

"Eeeehhhhh, shaddap now you people!" the same bartender from that morning shouted above the crowd. "Eeeehhhh, we have a new fighter tonight, just came into Terminus this morning. What? Yeah, yup yup. He's gonna fight or The Illustrious will have his head on the wall to pay for the room and meal. Who's up to challenge the human?"

"He's too puny for a real fight, let Orra have him!" came a shout from the crowd.

"Eeeehhhhh, yup yup, let Orra fight! Eh? What's that? Yeah, Orra," cackled the bartender.

Heishi stepped into the center of the circle of onlookers, wondering who Orra was and what the joke was. His question was soon answered as another fighter stepped into the ring. This one was female, and as such was allowed a top for her fighting "uniform." She stood around six feet tall and was of the same race of shark people that Hungry was. She was well built, although not compared to Hungry, and she had a snarl on her lips as she stepped into the ring. Scars covered her face and body and she appeared to be no stranger to the ring, although it was probable that she was not exactly a champion based on the number of scars.

"You's ready to die, human?" Orra asked as she flashed a mouth full of teeth.

The bartender stepped between the two: "Eeeehhh, you know the rules, Orra: this ain't a fight to the death. You know the Illustrious doesn't like wasting fighters!"

"What exactly are the rules?" Heishi asked, never taking his eyes off his opponent.

"Eeehhh, no weapons, no killing, first fighter knocked out or can't continue loses. Eeehh? Whassat? Oh yeah, and losers don't get paid."

As he finished speaking, the bartender looked around the room a few times as if searching for something or someone. He then let out a yelp and scurried out of the ring, muttering under his breath to himself the whole way.

As soon as he moved from between the combatants, Orra leaped into action, taking a swing at Heishi's head. Having watched her from the second she stepped into the ring, he was not caught off guard, and easily ducked the blow. He dropped to his right knee, shifted his weight from the hip, and delivered a punch directly to Orra's knee.

Howling in pain, Orra took a single step back, then moved forward again, putting the bulk of her body behind a kick aimed for Heishi's chest. He shifted to the left, allowing the kick to slide past his right shoulder, and turned into a left upper cut that caught Orra in the gut.

That's like punching a solid wall! I need to be more careful or I'm going to hurt myself…

As she fell back and rolled to the side from the punch, she dragged her leg across Heishi's shoulder and right side of his face. It was then he realized his mistake: the skin of her leg had been smooth as it slid past but pulling back the other direction it was rough and tore some of the skin from the side of his face and neck. As the blood flowed, the crowd whooped in excitement, causing Orra to spin back on him to evaluate the damage. At the sight of fresh blood, her eyes rolled back in her head a bit, and a line of spittle slid from the side of her mouth.

Great, the shark smelled blood in the water. This is gonna hurt…

She came on with reckless abandon, attempting to finish the job. But Heishi was no novice to battle, and as she ran toward him, he shifted back to the right and slid around her back, grabbing her small dorsal fin and pulling her off her feet. As her body slammed to the floor of the bar, he stepped out into a wide horse stance and punched her squarely in the side of her head with all the power he had left in him. A resounding crack sounded across the bar that could be heard in the street, and her head slumped to the side, unmoving.

All sound in the bar came to a sudden halt, and Heishi stood up and stepped off to the side. As everyone looked on, two dirty vagrant-looking men ran into the ring to drag the unconscious fighter out. As the first grabbed an arm, he stopped and looked at her chest, which was not moving. He signaled to the little bartender, waved them to remove her from the ring. As the crowd watched, a man in a hooded cloak slid from a table in the corner to Orra's side as they dragged her out. He turned his back to the crowd, and Heishi could see his arms moving as he inspected her. He turned toward the bartender and said something quietly, then moved back to his table.

"Eeehhh, this is what happens when you break the rules! Orra tried to kill this new human, and now she's dead. Eeeehhh, next fight!"

As cheers broke out across the bar, Hungry approached Heishi and signaled him out of the ring. "Hey, you's need to see the healer and get dressed. Now. Boss wants to sees you, and the Boss don't like waiting."

Heishi felt the wound on his face and

neck, wiped it with his hand, and replied, "I do not need a healer, it is just a scratch. Have some water and a towel sent to my room and I will clean up there as I get dressed."

"OK human. Don't be late. The Boss don't like waiting."

"Yeah, you mentioned that. I will be right down."

Heishi returned a short time later to the bar amidst another fight, this time between a tough looking dwarf and an elf. This place is out of control, I need to get home. Hungry was waiting for him and did not appear to be doing so patiently. He was escorted to a wall on the left side of the bar and a door slid open as they approached. They stepped through the wall and into an opulent office that was very much out of place from everything else he had witnessed thus far in Terminus.

Standing in front of a huge desk in the back of the office was the largest shark-man Heishi had seen yet. Towering over him at around eight feet tall, the shark-man was the most imposing figure he had seen in his life. He was dressed in full plate armor colored blood red, and a helmet sat on the desk beside him. His face resembled a great white shark, and his eyes were those of a predator sizing up his next meal. He held a wicked looking sword with a silver blade and a red edge in his right hand, resting easily with the tip on the floor in front of him. The sword was at least four feet long itself, which was impressive enough, except in his left hand he also had a shield that had to be at least four to five feet in diameter as well. The shield was black in color and had gold shark teeth the size of Heishi's fist facing out around the edge. In the center of the shield was a raised relief of a shark surrounded by clouds and with two rubies as eyes. There were battle scars on the shield, showing that he was no novice to battle.

A shark god of some type maybe? This has got to be the Illustrious one the bartender keeps mentioning. I better behave if I want to live through this meeting.

"Kneel before the boss, human!" Hungry spat at him.

Heishi realized he was gawking at this monster before him and was the only one in the room not bowing to the beast. Realizing his mistake, he promptly knelt to the floor, placed his sword out to his side, and bowed with his forehead to the floor. Appeased, the Boss nodded, and Hungry yanked Heishi back to his feet.

"Who are you, human? Why are you here with no money? Your clothes are nothing to look at, but that sword says you aren't a peasant and you fight well. Why are you in my bar?" the

Illustrious asked?

Heishi bowed from his waist and stood up straight again before replying, "Sir, may I ask how to properly address you? I can tell that you are a man whose reputation precedes him wherever he goes, but I am not from anywhere near here and must admit I am at a loss."

The Boss stared intently for several intense seconds before grinning, showing off a mouth full of razor-sharp teeth. "I am called by a lot of names. The Illustrious is my favorite, but only that worm at the bar calls me that. My men call me Boss. If you come to work for me, that is what you will call me. For now, as you have shown to be a man worth dealing with, you can call me Jim."

Heishi did well to not show his surprise at the simple name given. "Well, Jim, to be truthful, I was with some companions when we were caught up in a storm of red lightning. We were lifted into the air, then hurtled toward the ground again. I blacked out before hitting the ground, but when I awoke, I was on the other side of this mountain, but where I started there are no mountains. The guard at the gate mentioned 'planes of existence,' but I don't know what he is referring to. I am forever in your debt for allowing me food and shelter before I worked to earn it, and if you could assist me further in discovering what brought me here to your 'plane of existence' I would do whatever work necessary to pay for that help."

What's the worst he can do for telling the truth? Kill me and eat me? Well, yeah, I guess he could do that…

Jim paused and stared at him for a full minute before continuing. "I have heard of these different 'planes,' but I have never met anyone from one. Interesting. I made up my mind about you, human. I will give you everything you need to complete a task for me, and if you can do it, you will have all the gold you need to get your answers."

He looked at Hungry next. "You, go get this human some companions to go with him to get my Orb."

Hungry bowed again, and quietly left the room, leaving Heishi alone with Jim.

This guy clearly isn't afraid of me or anyone else.

"Sir, what is this Orb you need me to acquire for you?" Heishi asked.

"My men will give you a map. Follow it to the caves in the mountain, and there you will find a tribe of orcs who have stolen from me. Their chieftain holds an Orb of great power that I want back. If you can retrieve it for me, I will pay you and tell you where you can find your answers. If you cannot, then I will assume you are dead like the rest and find someone else to get it. This is your one chance, human. If you run, I will find you and use your bones to pick your flesh from my teeth."

Chapter 5 - The Companions

As Heishi reentered the bar, Hungry waived him to the back table where the man in the cloak had been sitting. There were now others at the table, although through the smoke-filled bar, he could not make them out. He headed around the edge of the crowd, who were cheering for the next fight in progress, and came to stand before the table. As he approached, Hungry snarled at him and walked away, back to whatever duties he was being kept from.

Taking a seat, Heishi recognized Shemoc across the table grinning at him. To his left was the oversized dwarf he had seen on the street, and to his right sat the cloaked figure.

"Heishi, good to see you. It appears you are a fighter after all. Orra was not given the credit she was due as a fighter because she was a female, but for a human to kill her with a punch has started rumors across town. I heard the rumors and came to see how you fared; apparently better than Orra, and with nothing but a scratch to show for it. Impressive."

Shenroc was smiling as he spoke, and the dwarf was as well. The cloaked man remained in shadows.

"May I introduce my associate Yutri, of the clan Wetree," Shenroc continued, gesturing toward the dwarf.

"You-tree?" Heishi asked.

"No, I'm a dwarf, not a tree, human," the over-sized dwarf responded. "My name is Yutri, of the clan Wetree."

"Forgive my ignorance, good dwarf," Heishi responded. "I have never met a dwarf before today, and then to meet one of your, uh, stature, put me off a bit. It is a pleasure to meet you."

"Stature?" asked Yutri.

"He means he expected you to be smaller, you oaf," answered Shenroc, whose smile turned into a full belly laugh. "I am sorry, Heishi, Yutri is not the sharpest blade in the armory, but he is a great warrior and a better friend. Just do not ask him to solve any puzzles for you."

"Is the clan Wetree a large clan?" Heishi inquired.

"Just me. I am my own clan. Dad was a dwarf, mom was a short giant, neither of them wanted me when I grew, so I started my own clan. Someday the clan Wetree will be the biggest clan ever." Yutri beamed, impressed with his ability to start his own clan.

Stifling a smile, the others at the table nodded, secretly taking joy in his choice of words.

Biggest clan ever. I'll say. He's an idiot but seems trustworthy.

All eyes turned toward the final member of the group, the cloaked man. An audible sigh came from under the hood, and the shadow spoke: "I will remove my hood for but a moment. It is important to look a man in his eyes to understand him, and of this I am aware. However, my presence in Terminus may not be taken well by some, as I am a shadow elf. My people are unnecessarily brutal and xenophobic, killing all who are not of our race in service to a dark deity. I have left my home underground for that reason but am not well received on the surface world. Big Jim allows me to work as a healer for his fights when I am in town if I remain hidden. You did not come see me after your fight with Orra..."

Heishi flinched but did not pull away as the cloaked man reached out a gloved hand and placed it on the side of his shredded neck. Warmth flowed through his neck, and when the stranger removed his hand, he reached up to touch the spot and was shocked to discover the skin no longer was torn from the shark skin.

Remarkable. Aki would be jealous.

As the cloaked man peeled back his hood,

the three at the table barely stifled a gasp. A head full of white hair was pulled back from his coal black face into a braid that fell over his left shoulder. Crimson eyes stared back not unkindly at Heishi, but with a hint of wariness. His features were that of a surface elf, with attractive, chiseled bone structure and clear complexion: with the single exception of the black skin. Shadows curled around his exposed skin as light from the lanterns in the room fell upon it, attempting to conceal him in shadow. After making eye contact with all at the table, he promptly returned his hood, reverting his face to obscurity.

"The name given me at birth does not matter, as I have left the evil of my people. Those who have looked past my heritage and known me on the surface have given me the name Di'eslo, and I am pleased to make your acquaintance. I will not allow death to take you, as it took your opponent in the ring this evening. She was an evil creature and unworthy of my efforts to revive her."

"Well met, Di'eslo, Yutri, and Shenroc. I am Heishi. Shenroc met me at the gate and is aware of my plight, but I feel it necessary to inform the rest of you before you agree to this journey. I have been ripped from my world, my plane of existence, and thrust into this one. I had four companions with me and have yet to find them upon entering this plane. Jim has promised to give me gold enough to find answers if I retrieve an Orb of unknown power that was stolen from him by the orcs living in the mountain. We are supposed to receive a map from his men that will lead us to the cave entrance. If anyone is uncomfortable with this, now is your time to walk away."

Shenroc chuckled as Heishi finished speaking. "Do you think any of us were given a choice in accompanying you? Big Jim runs all of Terminus, and if we do not assist you, he will kill us as well as our families. The speech was excellent but let us go and attempt to cheat death by the people of my father and discover riches untold."

As they were chatting, Hungry returned to the table. "Boss says you's need to go to the map shop. Tell the guy the Boss says give you the map. It opens in the morning, and you's need to be there early. The Boss don't like waiting."

"I believe you have mentioned that. Where do I find this map shop?" Heishi inquired.

"Not here. Find it yousself, I ain't got time to babysit no humans." Hungry grinned and promptly walked away.

"Well, you heard him. We can meet here again early in the morning, grab some food from the bar, and head out. Jim said he would outfit me with proper travelling gear since I have been caught somewhat unprepared for this journey. Is there somewhere I can purchase some gear and armor...on credit?" Heishi looked sheepish at the last statement.

"I know a place just around the corner. The shop keeper loves me," Yutri said, then smiled, blushed a little, and immediately stopped talking.

"Ok, we will meet here in the morning, stock up on supplies, then see what this world has to offer." Heishi looked at each man at the table in turn. "Do not worry, I have some experience in battle, and I do not plan on losing anyone on this team. Get some sleep, tomorrow could get interesting."

Before the sun rose, Heishi was sitting at a table eating a breakfast of bread and fish soup and wondering if that was all there was to eat in this town. By mentioning Big Jim to the bartender, he was able to acquire some extra loaves of bread and a backpack to put them in.

Same bartender. Does this weird little guy ever sleep? Or are there more of them back there just taking turns? Nah, that guy is an individual...

Shenroc and Yutri arrived together a short time later, and Di'eslo slid through the door just as the first rays of light began to filter through the cracked, filthy windows. Yutri was wearing the same plate armor Heishi had previously seen him in but was now wearing a matching helmet with the face guard raised. Hanging on his left hip was a massive war hammer that would take both hands for a normal man to wield. Strapped to his back was a large silver shield with a hammer and anvil engraved in the center and a scorched mark burned across the center. He caught Heishi admiring the shield. "Mithril. Stops everything, even dragon fire. No matter what I do I cannot get that burn mark off though. The ladies love it." He flashed a lewd grin to Heishi and turned back to his food.

Shenroc was dressed in the same leather armor he previously wore, but on top he added a hauberk that also appeared to be mithril. He still carried the wicked looking daggers at his sides, but across his back he also bore a claymore with a leather wrapped handle and a kris blade. The sword, too, appeared to be made of mithril.

I guess it's good to be friends with dwarves, if the mythical tales are true about dwarves and mithril. Given everything I have seen so far, I can only imagine that many of the myths and fantasy books I have read are based in truth.

Given the hour of the morning, the bar was empty and Di'eslo had his cloak pulled off and laid across the back of his chair as he ate.

Heishi

He wore a set of black plate mail, and on his hip, he wore a nasty-looking flail. The handle and chain of the flail were solid black, and while the ball at the end of the chain was also black, the spikes shone purple with inner power. Beside the table leg rested his shield, which was also black in color with a purple spider web that covered the face of the shield and glowed with the same inner light as the spikes on his flail.

Each carried a large pack stuffed with food and other supplies for the journey. Having spoken with some of the guards the previous night, Heishi assumed it would not be a long journey to the cave itself, but once underground no one knew the extent of the tunnels. Having a shadow elf and a half-orc in the party would be useful in such an environment.

The companions quickly finished their meals and headed out to the street, which was just beginning to stir. The map shop was only a few blocks away, and the armor shop Yutri recommended was a little further toward the front gate. They headed quickly through the quiet streets, and came to the front of the map shop, which was aptly named "Maps."

This guy is a simpleton, has a sense of humor, or I'm about to have another interesting morning.

Heishi opened the front door and heard a bell jingle in the back. He faced a small shop with four rows of shelves covered with round cylinders presumably filled with maps of different sorts. To his far left, the shelves were older and covered in layers of dust; the shelves on his right were newer, contained less dust, and were not entirely filled with maps. The rear of the shop had a U-shaped counter with curtains in the back-right corner, through which appeared the shop owner. He was able to control his surprise at finding a goblin in a robe and carrying a scroll walking to the counter. The goblin stood around five feet tall, with green skin, oversized pointed ears, black eyes, and a mouth full of crooked teeth. The goblin stared at the visitors, waiting for them to announce why they disturbed him.

"Sir, we are searching for a map that will lead us to a cave system on the mountain where the orcs live," Heishi started to explain.

"Yeah, I can get what you need," the goblin stated in a nasal voice. "To make the map, I will need inkless ink, the skin of a dragon, and the blood of a freshly killed orc. That's important, it can't be more than an hour old. Bring me this and I can make your map."

"Inkless ink? Skin of a dragon? Fresh orc blood? Big Jim said you would have the map for us," Shenroc bristled at the absurdity of the request.

"Oooohhh, Big Jim. Why didn't you say so, human? Of course, of course, I have the map,

I have it right back here. You can't be coming into my place of business saying you want things when it is Big Jim who wants them!" The goblin disappeared behind the curtain and the companions heard papers rustling and heavy objects crashing to the floor. A few moments later, the goblin reappeared, smoothing his robes and attempting to appear calm. "Here's the map, free of charge. You won't be telling Big Jim about the inkless ink thing, right? That was a joke between friends..."

Di'eslo reached out and took the map, rolling it out on the counter to ensure it was legitimate. "Not a difficult map to follow, but the road could be fraught with danger before we even reach the cave."

"I guess we better find out how much the armor shop keeper actually loves Yutri, I will need something to keep me alive," Heishi stated, then looked at Di'eslo: "No offense. I am positive you will keep us alive, of course."

"But of course..."

The companions left the map shop and walked three blocks over to a shop named, "Orra's Armor." Heishi looked at Yutri, who nodded that this was indeed the correct place. Shenroc slapped Yutri on the side of his head, waited a minute, and Yutri finally understood why everyone was staring at him. A flush of color reached his cheeks as he stammered,

"Well, the owner USED to love me. I bet we get a good deal on anything in the shop today..."

They entered the store, which was empty. After searching the back they came to the realization that Orra was the sole proprietor of the establishment, and her untimely demise left all her belongings to Heishi. Shenroc explained to the newcomer that anything belonging to your opponent killed fairly in battle then became the property of the victor.

Looks like I'm in the blacksmith business. Just what I always wanted...

All eyes turned to Heishi as Shenroc finished his explanation, reminding him of kids in a candy store waiting for permission to get anything they desired. He furrowed his brow for a moment as he decided whether he should keep everything to sell later if he was stuck in this place, then realized there would not be a later if this team died in the caves. A grin creased his lips as he slowly nodded, "Yes, you may take any gear that you can use, free of charge. If we live through this, we will decide what to do with the shop, as I am no blacksmith."

With a whoop, the companions began to ransack the shop for anything that could assist in not becoming a meal for an orc. Heishi was outfitted with leather breeches and shirt and a chain mail hauberk like Shenroc's of high-quality steel, albeit not of the same caliber as mithril. He kept his katana, but also added a strong short bow and quiver of arrows to his arsenal and filled his pack with a bedroll, some rope, and other miscellaneous gear based on his extensive survival training and medieval video game playing. He also found a forest green cloak with a hood that would cover his facial features well and would assist in camouflage should the need arise. When he was done all that remained of his previous dress was his jungle boots, katana, and the pistol in a thigh holster on his leg. The rest were able to stock up on extra arrows and a piece of armor here and there, but the gear Orra had available could not compare to mithril.

As Heishi was searching her private area in the back hoping to find some gloves, he discovered a panel in the wall that was almost hidden from view. He pushed lightly on the panel, and it slid open to reveal her personal treasures. As he surveyed the stash, he was drawn to a ring in the back. It was a simple gold band with a strip of emerald running around the center, and when he picked it up, he felt a slight tingle. As he examined the ring, he began to understand that this ring would apply poison to anything he wished if he placed his hand on it. Sliding the ring onto his ring finger on his right hand, it shrank to fit him perfectly.

I could get used to this. Zatus will have his work cut out for him to stay ahead of tech like this!

He completed his rifling of her stash, and except for some diamonds and other valuables, he determined that nothing else would be of use on this trip. He replaced the panel in the wall, ensured it was hidden again, and walked out to the main shop where his companions were finished searching for gear themselves.

"That was productive. Secure the front door so we can sell this place when we return. Time to make the green grass grow," Heishi said with a chuckle. Noticing the looks on the faces of his team, he explained, "It is something said to Soldiers in training. The instructor asks, 'What makes the green grass grow?' The Soldiers reply, 'Blood makes the green grass grow!' I say it to my team before every mission."

"That is good, Heishi. Let us go make the green grass grow," grinned Shenroc.

Chapter 6:
The Discovery

The sun was getting high in the sky as the companions walked out the gates of Terminus. Shenroc explained as they walked that the gates were open during the day with guards in the towers questioning travelers, and the mantrap was only used during hours of darkness when respectable people were not attempting to enter the city. He smiled warmly at Heishi as he said, "respectable people," and with a wink said, "There are, however, a few exceptions."

Following the map acquired from the goblin, Di'eslo lead the group to the East as they exited the gates, which lead them the opposite direction from where Heishi had arrived. The day was not hot, the sun was bright, and the fresh air put each of them in an exceptional mood. A short way down the road, the map pointed the companions to a foot path that was mostly overgrown and shaded with large trees. According to the map, this path would take them to the far side of the mountain, where there were two entrances to the orc lair, one high on the mountain and another by the side of a lake.

Di'eslo removed his hood and gloves when the gates were out of sight, reveling in the shadows of the trees, and began to question Heishi about the exact circumstances of his arrival. Heishi explained briefly the purpose of his antiterrorism team and gave a few unclassified details of the threat he had been trying to neutralize. Di'eslo was especially interested when he explained the airplane he flew in before the jump, and that he was able to survive falling from such a great height.

"If we live, I will take you to the place I landed and show you my parachute. The material is very light, made of silk, and catches the air to slow the Paratrooper as he falls to Earth," described Heishi.

"Remarkable. I want to know of this Art," Di'eslo breathed with wide eyes.

"Art? What art?"

"The Art, your ability from the gods to fall from the sky and live. The Art is how I healed your wound last night; I tapped into the energy around you to reconstruct your skin as it was before."

"Ahh, so the Art is another word for magic?" Heishi inquired.

Di'eslo laughed heartily at that question. "No, human, magic is not real, at least not in the sense that there are secret words or incantations to learn. I do not believe the gods are real either, or at least I have never met one to change my mind. No, the Art just refers to learning how energy surrounds us all, and some can become attuned to it in special ways. My attunement came in the form of healing and a select few offensive abilities. Some can throw fireballs from an empty hand, some can make the ground shake, others use lightning. It is not 'magic,' as you say, it is simply understanding the energy surrounding us and shaping it to our will."

"Can items be attuned using this energy?"

"Yes, there are items of remarkable power that are imbued with the Art. I happen to have a few of these items myself but will never tell what they do. I assume you found something at the shop of Orra. Keep it to yourself, as these items are highly sought after and have caused the death of many an unexpecting traveler." Di'eslo glanced down at the ring Heishi now wore. "Some items seem to be more difficult to hide than others, of course."

Deciding a subject change was in order, Heishi steered the conversation a different way. "I have told you of my world but have yet to learn anything about this one. I know the town was Terminus, but do not even know what this world is called. You seem to be well educated, anything you can explain about planes of existence would also be much appreciated."

"This world is known as Kartos. There are many planes, and few understand more than our own. Those who are trained in the Art are more aware of the planes and the shifts between them than others." Heishi had been watching ahead for danger as they talked, but his head snapped to the side at the mention of shifts between planes. "No, human, you are not the first to be caught in a shift between the planes. I do not understand such things, or if there is a way to return, so do not stare at me like this. I simply know that these things happen sometimes, and that others may be able to help with your plight."

The conversation was meant to help the time pass, but it effectively distracted Heishi from scanning his sector of the path for danger. Without warning, an arrow thunked into the ground between Heishi and Di'eslo, and another stuck in between Shenroc and Yutri behind them. As each reached for his weapon, a shrill whistle sounded in the trees behind them, and a voice that seemed to come from everywhere at once said, "The first to draw a weapon is the first to die."

The companions slowly moved their hands away from their weapons, and a man wearing clothes made from animal hides and a dark brown cloak eased out of the trees to the right. He slowly approached the group, watching them cautiously for any signs of movement. He stopped just out of sword range from Heishi and grinned. "This here is our path. If you want to leave alive, it will cost you. Toss your weapons onto the path behind you, then step forward and drop your gold and jewelry. If you do as you are told, no one will get hurt. If you do not, well, none of you will leave this place."

As he spoke, Heishi watched four others dressed similarly closing in to form a circle around the group. Two of the others closing in had bows with arrows knocked and pointed toward the group, the other two were outfitted with a sword and shield, and all five had a nervous air about them. He inhaled and let out a breath, then slowly scanned the trees where the intruders had appeared. As the wind blew, he noticed a section of a tree to his half left where the leaves did not move with the rest: a tree blind.

Either there is still one more out there covering this group or I missed one of the archers climbing out of a tree.

Nudging Di'eslo and slightly nodding in the direction of the blind, he hoped the elf would understand. Turning his head toward Heishi, he winked to show he saw it as well.

"Good sir, you know this is a treacherous area. We cannot give you our weapons, and we are but poor travelers with not much gold. We would gladly share our food rations with you to avoid an untimely death, but we cannot accommodate your request to give up our weapons," Heishi explained.

If the man was surprised, it did not show as an evil smile crept across his face. "Then you all die."

Expecting that response, Heishi moved first, pulling his pistol from the thigh holster and aiming between his eyes. No one present expected the following explosion as he pulled the trigger, instantly killing the speaker. Wanting to conserve ammunition as he would not be able to purchase more in this place, he used the stunned silence to holster his weapon and slide the katana from his back, not yet igniting the electricity of the blade. Di'eslo was the next to move, simultaneously pulling his shield from his back and snatching the flail from his side while turning toward the next attacker. Shenroc and Yutri recovered quickly and both had weapons in hand and were moving toward the closest attackers to them.

Di'eslo moved toward his opponent rapidly, the shadows curling from his skin as his anger flared. The man in front of him saw the shadow elf coming and his face paled. He swung a two-handed club at the elf as he tried to back away, and the blow glanced easily off his shield. The first swing of his flail was meant to cripple the man at the knees, but he was back tracking quickly enough that Di'eslo only landed a glancing blow on the man's calf. That snapped him out of his shock at seeing an evil elf coming at him, and he spun away from the hit and came back with a straight shot to the face with his club.

The speed of the attack caught the elf off guard, and all he could do was shift his head to the left and accept the glancing blow to the right side of his head. He felt the blood flow a bit but had no time to worry about that as the man retracted his club and came at him with an overhead swing meant to crush the smaller elf. Di'eslo reached into his innate power inherent to his race and stepped into the shadow of the tree beside him, disappearing as the club swung down and smashed into the ground where he had been standing. As the confused attacker looked on dumbly, the elf reappeared behind him and followed up with a swing of his own directly above his head, burying the made into his skull. As the man crumpled to the ground, Di'eslo took a moment to heal his wound, then turned to assist his companions.

Shenroc was embattled with an attacker of his own, who did not appear afraid of the half-orc in front of him. His opponent had loosed his arrow, which was now protruding from Shenroc's left shoulder, then switched to a rusted long sword and a dented shield. The two were squared off, and if Shenroc felt any pain in his shoulder he was not letting on. His eyes were bloodshot, and flecks of white showed in the edges of his mouth where his tusks protruded. With a primal roar, he swung his claymore at his opponent, whose wooden shield shattered as he blocked the strike. A look of shock appeared on his face as he tried to counter with an attack of his own, but Shenroc did not relent his attack. Pulling his sword back to the left as he followed through his strike, he brought it back around in a figure eight motion and cleaved the head from his opponent with a clean strike. His bloodlust not sated, he brought the sword above his head for a third and final strike, which cut through bone and tissue like butter as he removed the sword arm from the bandit before his body dropped in the dirt.

While this was taking place, Yutri sang a battle song in Dwarvish as he whipped his battle hammer around like a toy. His opponent, the second archer, attempted to stay out of range of the wild behemoth dwarf, alternately running and turning to fire another missile at Yutri. Each time an arrow took flight, the massive mithril shield was there to promptly pick it from the air, and a swing of the hammer would have the archer moving again. The dwarf laughed with each failed attempt, which served to demoralize his opponent who had come to the realization that his situation was untenable. He moved further and further up the path, trying to angle toward the trees where the hidden blind was located, but Yutri was there every step of the way pressing his attack.

On his side of the melee, Heishi was engaged with the final visible bandit, an elf who stood a head taller than he and had the extra reach to go with it. The elf had produced a short sword in his primary hand and a dagger in the other and proved adept at using both fluidly. A quick stab came from his left side as the bandit attempted to impale him with the sword, but he was able to pick the attack off cleanly and remained balanced to spin out of range of the gleaming dagger that followed in on his right. Neither came on recklessly, both understanding the considerable skill of his opponent.

Heishi feinted left, then swung his blade over his right shoulder and attacked low, aiming for the left leg of his attacker. The dagger was there in a flash, turning the blade aside so the tip barely slid across the leather breeches of the bandit. His blade was exquisite, and would normally rip through leather pants, but he did not leave a scratch with the cut. The elf grinned, noticing his frustration, and flew into an intricate combination of cuts with both blades, moving Heishi back a step or two with each fluid movement. He stayed slightly ahead of the routine, picking off each attack cleanly and looking for an opening but not finding any.

After several of these combinations, the elf attempted to stab Heishi in the belly with his dagger, but he was able to shift his hips to the left, use the side of his blade to slap the short sword out wide, and with the dagger still coming toward where he had been a moment before he brought his blade back to the center and slashed up from the hip. Hoping his attacker would be cut in half as the rat monster was, his shock was complete when the leather completely protected the elf from his attack, forcing him to retreat and regain his footing. His shock apparent, the elf attacked in a daring attempt to finish the duel, but he did not understand the nature of the blade he faced. Heishi parried the first attack of the short sword, and as he brought his blade up for a killing strike activated the green lightning of his blade. The green sparks distracted the elf for a split second, which was all Heishi needed to bring the blade back across and stab through the armor and into the heart of his opponent. The shock froze on his face as the elf died, the blade sticking clean through his chest and out his back.

A shout rose from the tree blind as the blade activated, and the bandit Yutri was chasing looked over his shoulder to see why his lookout was breaking silence. The dwarf laughed as he brought his war hammer over his head and hurled it into the side of his head, knocking him to the side as his head caved in at the impact. Yutri quickly retrieved his hammer and faced the tree blind from behind his magnificent shield, ready to face more incoming arrows.

Di'eslo walked cautiously to Shenroc, keeping his shield in front of him as well, and pointed to the arrow in his chest. Shenroc looked down, laughed insanely, and jerked the arrow free from his chest, causing blood to flow freely. He appeared not to notice the blood, and turned toward the tree, ready to face the next threat. Di'eslo sighed and put his hand out toward the wound, then watched as a blue mist reached out from his palm and began to knit the muscle and tissue back together while Shenroc began to run.

Not to be outdone, Heishi sprinted to catch up to Shenroc, and the two barreled down on the tree blind, oblivious to the danger. As they approached the area, the blind became apparent, with cut bushes propped on piled up logs starting at ground level and reaching up into the trees to give an elevated position.

Shenroc broke off to the left side while Heishi came up on the right, and as he was about to enter the blind a man stepped out. He wore a cloak of dark green like the one Heishi had chosen but leaves and moss had been attached to the cloak to form a type of ghillie suit. The man held a sniper rifle by the barrel in his left hand and slipped it to the ground as he stepped out into the light and raised both hands in a nonthreatening manner. Shenroc roared in victory as he came behind the man, ready to eliminate him, but Heishi gasped and shouted "Shenroc, NO!" as the bandit slid the hood from his face.

Against all odds, standing before him, stood Staff Sergeant Tiane. His appearance was more rugged than when the team had jumped from the plane; he had grown a thick beard, and had clearly spent some time in the sun, but Heishi would know his sniper anywhere. He dropped his sword, immediately dousing the electrical energy coursing through it, and grabbed Tiane in a bear hug.

"My boy, good to see you! How did you get here? When did you get here? What are you doing with bandits?" Heishi started asking questions faster than Tiane could answer them.

"Master--"

Heishi cut him off before he could finish the sentence with a shake of his head. "Just

Heishi here, my brother."

"Fair enough. What do you remember of our jump?" Tiane asked tentatively. "I just want to know if I am crazy or not."

The two took a seat behind the blind as the remainder of the companions kept watch. Heishi went through what he remembered of the storm, of raising into the sky, then plummeting back to earth. He described the silver light shining from Zatus' eyes and finished by saying he counted three parachutes before he blacked out. Tiane nodded through the whole story, confirming this was his recollection as well, including only counting three parachutes. He then briefly recapped the last few days, his experience in the bar, the mission Jim had given, and what Di'eslo had explained to him about planes of existence.

"And that leads up to your friends attacking me on the path. What are you doing with bandits?" Heishi asked sternly.

"Top, I don't know if you will believe this. I still don't believe it. But I'll give it a shot."

Chapter 7 – The Sniper

As Tiane plummeted to Earth, he saw the silver light shining from Zatus' eyes. He frantically reached for his friend's ripcord to make sure he landed safely, but Zatus beat him to it. Seeing his friend safe, he reached for his own and counted three other parachutes as his unfurled. Horrified, he saw CPT Aldith burn in and bounce off the ground, parachute still not deployed. Although he did not like her anyway, he could not help but feel a twinge of sorrow watching her die that way: then he saw a bright flash of red light and everything went black.

When he awoke, he was hanging in his harness from the branch of a tall tree in the middle of a forest. As he looked around to get his bearings, he saw a mountain poking out above the trees in front of him, the top of which was shrouded in clouds. It was light, but most of the area around him was hidden in shadows. He looked down, and there were bushes around the base of the tree, but he estimated it was no more than fifteen feet down.

"Ronin One, this is Ronin Four."
Nothing.

"Ronin Six, Ronin Four, come in."

Still nothing.

"Any Ronin element, this is Ronin Four, come in."

Technically this was impossible according to Zatus. His communicators had worked across the world in any environment and had never once glitched. It was possible that the lightning fried it, so Tiane decided not to panic yet, but he needed to find a way out of the tree soon before he lost all feeling in his legs.

He pulled the handle on his reserve parachute, ejecting it and watching it fall beneath him to the ground below. Slowly, he unhooked his chest strap, then his right leg strap, wrapped his right leg around the suspension lines for his reserve for support, then disconnected his left leg strap. The backpack with his rifle and ammunition was tangled in branches of the tree, so he cut it loose, watched it drop beneath him, then slid carefully down the suspension lines of his reserve to the ground.

Upon retrieving his pack, he put his rifle together and looked for any traces of his team. He found none, and as the sun seemed to be setting, decided to make a camp to stay close to his landing site. All thoughts of his mission were gone, as he clearly was nowhere near the theme park, so as he started cutting tree branches to make a shelter for the night, he just hoped the rest of the team was able to stop that bomb. He put together a quick shelter with a floor lifted a few inches off the ground to keep him dry and keep animals away with a roof made of strange looking leaves he had never seen before. He dug a small fire pit, collected some dry branches as kindling and a few logs he hoped would burn, and surveyed his small camp: it would suffice for a short-term solution.

Tiane reached into his backpack and pulled out the fourteen-inch wooden handles. He stared at the handles for a minute, then mentally commanded the blades to spring from the handles completing the kamas, the sickles, that Zatus had crafted for him. He put them through a few moves to loosen up his shoulders, then ignited the blades into green flames with a thought. He had no idea how Zatus did these things, especially being able to color the fire green, but he really loved these weapons. He smiled at the thought of Zatus and his inventions, then released the flames and slid the kamas into their specially designed holsters on his thighs.

The sun was setting behind the mountain as he slid into the shadows with his rifle to find his dinner. It did not take him long to find fresh tracks in the dirt close to his camp, although he could not figure out what type of animal had made them. After cautiously following the tracks for a way, he noticed the bushes ahead rustling although there was no wind. Stealthily moving through the brush, he found a tree with low hanging branches that would serve to get him above the limited visibility caused by the scrub for a better view of his target.

Hanging on a branch in the tree, Tiane realized how dark the woods had become while he stalked this animal. With no stars visible through the trees above, he was in complete darkness. The animal could still be heard moving but the bushes were no longer visible. He did not have his night vision scope as the operation was to take place during the day, and now Tiane was regretting his decision to pack light.

He stared intently into the darkness, focusing on the sound, and as he did so he felt himself becoming slightly lightheaded. It was as if he could feel the darkness around him as something tangible, folding around the trees, the bushes, and the animal he was planning to eat. As he focused, the woods became lighter, and soon he was able to see shades of grey all around him, and then was startled when his prey appeared before him. He could see the heat signature of what appeared to be a huge rat as if he was staring through a thermal scope.

Blinking a few times to ensure he was seeing correctly, he eased his rifle to his shoulder, slowed his breathing, lined up his shot, and slowly squeezed the trigger. Through his scope he could see the head of the animal explode, and the headless body dropped to the ground, blood oozing from where its head once was and creating a pool of hot blood in the dirt. Tiane slid the bolt of his rifle open slowly, catching the cooling brass casing and easing it into the sleeve pocket of his shirt, then chambered another round.

Easing himself lightly to the ground, he prowled through the darkness until he stood next to the corpse. The body was quickly cooling, which was distorting his thermal vision of it, but he was convinced the beast was, in fact, a rat, although it was almost five feet long. He removed his black dagger from his boot and commenced field dressing the rat, separating meat from bone and organs, then followed his earlier path through the darkness to his camp.

A short time later, with a small fire cooking his meal, Tiane finally had time to reflect on the occurrences of this day. He had multiple combat deployments in Iraq and Afghanistan before joining Ronin Team, as well as a few that technically never happened, and as a sniper he was used to being alone. However, there were still those times, like now, where he could not help but let his mind wander, and the loneliness set in. Typically, the first few days were not so bad: it is nice to get some peace and quiet to offset the explosions, but in these hours of quiet it was hard not to miss friends and family.

Tiane had no living relatives, just like everyone else on the team. It made packing up and leaving on a moment's notice that much easier. But Ronin Team had become like a family to him. He really saw Heishi as a father type figure, Zatus was more of a brother to him than anyone he had ever met in his life, and Aki was like that crazy uncle that no one talked about but always brought you the coolest presents: usually the kind that explode if you use them properly. He sat in the dark and wondered where his family was: why no one was answering his repeated attempts on the communicator, and if any of them had survived the freak storm.

Most of all he wondered where he was and how he got here. Deployments were easy. He always had intel on the area before insertion, he had maps, and he had contingency plans. For the first time he was truly alone and felt lost. He needed to come up with a plan to get out of this mess, and for a moment he slipped into utter despair. As the tears formed, he reached into his memory to his survival training and remembered that the best way to push through this was to start planning his rescue. He finished his meal of roasted rat as he plotted his next steps to get out of the situation he was in and fell into a fitful sleep.

After a week of scouting the surrounding area and returning to his camp each night, he awoke as the sun was breaking over the horizon to the sound of a twig breaking just outside his camp. Remembering the size of the rodents he had been killing each night, Tiane eased the handles of his kamas from their thigh holsters, preparing to be attacked by a wild animal. His rifle was on his makeshift bed beside him, but his pistol was still in his backpack and would create unwanted noise to unzip the pack.

He slowly rolled to his stomach while watching his camp through the open side of his shelter. As a sniper he had been trained to move slowly and silently, and he took pride in mastering his craft. Silently he watched the open area, a single bead of sweat forming on his head as he consciously controlled his breathing. He would not be taken by surprise.

Occasionally he heard movement in the bushes on his left side, but whatever was out there was moving carefully as well, apparently aware of his presence. His patience finally paid off, and a man crept slowly into the edge of the clearing. He stood about medium height and had a slight build, but was hunched over, moving like a hunter tracking his prey. His dark brown cloak and animal hide breeches and tunic blended well with the trees behind him, which would make it difficult for a normal person to see him, but Tiane was not a normal person. He watched silently as the man moved into the camp, an arrow knocked in his bow with a slight bit of tension on the string, and he came to a stop on the other side of the fire pit which had burned out in the night leaving nothing but hot coals. His eyes were visible under the hood of the cloak, and Tiane could see them scanning for him.

In a swift movement, Tiane leapt from the shelter, simultaneously enacting the blades and bringing the emerald colored flames to life. Before the intruder was aware of his presence, Tiane was behind him with a burning kama blade to his throat. There was a moment of utter silence as the shock of his appearance settled on the man, and then he slowly reached his hands out to his sides and dropped his bow with the arrow still knocked.

"Who are you, and what are you doing?" Tiane hissed quietly. "And keep it quiet, if I think you are calling for help, I will remove your head."

"My name is Jurian," the man stammered. "I heard thunder from a clear sky last night, and when I came out to investigate this morning, I followed a blood trail and footprints from a butchered rat in the woods to this place. I did not mean to cause you alarm, but we do not get many travelers in this region due to the dangers, so I assumed the worst." As he whispered, he relaxed a bit. "I must tell you, friend, that there are four deadly archers in the bushes with arrows pointed at you. We mean you no harm, but if you kill me it will be the last thing you do."

Tiane eased his grip slightly but did not let go of Jurian. As he glanced around the clearing to verify the story he was told of archers, he was able to confirm three of the four. Extinguishing the flames of his kama, he slowly moved the blade away and released his prisoner. "I expect your men to come out where I can see them. Make no mistake, I can still kill you where you stand before an arrow can reach me."

"Fair enough, stranger," Jurian replied as he waved his arms to invite his companions to step forward. "He is safe, men, do him no harm," he called over his shoulder. He reached his hand toward Tiane and looked him in the eye, "As I said, my name is Jurian, a simple man attempting to survive in a cruel world. May I have the pleasure of knowing your name?"

"Call me Tiane, and it is a pleasure." As he spoke, he retracted the blades of his kama and returned them to the holsters on his thighs, reaching forward to grasp the hand Jurian held forth.

"Well, Master Tiane, what brings you to this place forsaken by the gods?"

Tiane began to answer, but it stopped in his throat as he glanced to his side to see an elf standing next to him. He tried to recover quickly, but could not keep from staring at the elf, who stared back at him quizzically.

"Jurian, this human acts as if he has never seen a woodland elf before," the elf chuckled. His voice was calm and sounded like running water, soothing Tiane into a sense of trust with the elf.

"Master Tiane, may I introduce Eogaon, of the woodland elves. May we assume you do not meet many elves in your realm?"

Never taking his eyes from Eogaon, Tiane shook his head slightly. "No, never. Umm, forgive me, but realm? I'm not sure where I am. Last I knew I was in Florida."

The group surrounding him exchanged glances before Jurian looked back at Tiane. "Florida? I have never heard of this realm. How did you come to be here? Speak quickly man, before my companions decide you are a spy and execute you."

Tiane slid his hands back to the handles of his kama. "That would be unwise, I am no spy. I was with my team, and there was a freak storm that came out of nowhere. There was red lightning, we were lifted in the air, then hurtled toward the ground, and I woke up in this place. I have no idea where I am, who you are, or why anyone would want to spy on you. I simply want to link back up with my team and be out of this place. I already told you, if you want to make a move, you die first."

At the mention of red lightning, a look of recognition crossed Eogaon's face and he nodded. Seeming content with that answer, Jurian motioned for Tiane to come with them. "Come, we have better food than rodent, and if you are a hunter you will find a place among us while we discern what happened to your friends."

Picking up his pack from inside his shelter, Tiane started off into the woods behind the group. He kept a watchful eye out for landmarks as they lead him deeper into the woods and further from the mountain. He was sure they were trying to confuse him, as they changed direction regularly, switched back on trails they had already walked, and after an hour or so of walking they came upon a small camp. Tiane looked to the mountain and discerned they had travelled less than a kilometer from their original location, although they had walked closer to four by his pace count.

Jurian waved him over and pulled up a

seat on a log next to the fire pit in the middle of the camp. "Here is the situation as I see it, Tiane. You clearly know how to survive in the wild. I do not know how you killed that rat, or where you come from, but if you are looking for a safe place to sleep at night you may stay here with us. We stay to ourselves, hunt for food, and avoid interaction with everyone out there." He waved his hand toward the mountain and back again. "If they do not bother us, we do not bother them. If you work and provide food, you are welcome to stay. If not, we will take you back to where we found you and leave you there."

The feeling of loneliness crept back into Tiane each time Jurian mentioned him leaving. A plan developed in his mind to stay here and search for civilization while he hunted, testing his communicator every day to see if his team would respond. He reached his hand out to Jurian: "where do I sleep?"

"That was three months ago, Top. I tried to radio the team every day. I searched the area around the camp when I went out to hunt, and never saw anything but wild animals. You wouldn't believe the animals here, Top. Those rats are the least of the weird things I have seen, but you are the first people. I switched to using a bow to hunt to conserve ammo because I have no idea how to get more out here, and some of these things will make your blood curl if you hunt it with a long bow.

This morning, Jurian, the one you shot, came running into camp. He said there were invaders on the path, and that we should get ready to fight for our lives. Something never sat right with me about that guy anyway: he would disappear with one or two of the others for a day or two at a time and when he returned, they would all huddle together and there would be a lot of whispering. When you shot him, I almost put a bullet in you, but I saw him reach for his weapon first. I was trying to figure out who else had a gun out here when I saw your sword light up, and I knew somehow that my companions had instigated the fight. And here we are." Tiane shook his head as he finished, clearly overwhelmed by his own story.

"Welcome back, son. We will figure this out. Come on, let me introduce you to my team and go see if your buddies there have anything worth scavenging."

Chapter 8 – The Path

After introductions were made, the group made their way back to the path where the bodies of the slain lay. Each member rifled through the belongings of their kill, taking extra arrows and knives. Other than the elf, who Heishi now new as Eogaon, the weapons used by the bandits were second rate at best. Heishi acquired the dagger the elf had used in his offhand, which was exceptionally made. Shenroc peered at the blade jealously, "That blade is of elvish design. It would appear this one lived with his people in the past, as it is near impossible to come across elvish blades outside the realm of elves. Consider yourself fortunate, my friend, you have received a treasure."

Picking up the short sword and inspecting it, he realized it was of a similar design to the dagger. Smiling, he put it through a few attack routines, marveling at the light weight and superb balance of the blade. He flipped the sword in the air and caught the blade, holding the handle out to Shenroc. "I have no need for a short sword, you take this one," he said as his smile broke into a full grin.

"I have no use for a sword that small, my friend, but the gesture is appreciated." It was difficult to tell through his green skin, but Heishi swore Shenroc was blushing a bit as he gracefully refused the offer. Not wanting to embarrass his friend further, he removed the sheath from the dead elf, slid the blade into it, and attached it to his pack.

"There is no need to leave a fine blade out here for a bandit to find, right?" Heishi quipped as he completed the action.

Heishi continued to search and felt drawn to a spot on the left forearm of the body, where he discovered a set of three throwing knives in a carrier hidden beneath the sleeve. He removed one of the knives and felt the same sensation as when he discovered the ring he now wore. Focusing on the blade, he knew it was imbued with something but could not discern what it was. Not wanting to lose this treasure, he removed the case for the knives and strapped it to his own forearm. A wave of understanding flowed over him as he cinched the buckle tight on his arm, and on a whim, he threw the knife he was holding and embedded it into a nearby tree. Focusing his attention on the knife in the tree, he was shocked to see it appear back in the sheath next to the other three.

"Next time, any elf we kill is mine," Shenroc laughed as he watched the knife reappear in the sheath. "You have been here for three days and already have more powerful weapons than most. I consider myself lucky to have made your acquaintance early, my friend." He slapped Heishi on the back and turned to the rest of the group. "It would appear these robbers had nothing of interest to us, except for him," he said pointing his thumb over his shoulder to the dead elf. "Shall we continue on to see what treasures the orcs have in store for us?"

The party set off once more, with Shenroc and Yutri out front, leading the way down the path and watching for danger. Di'eslo walked in the middle of the formation, several paces behind the two in the front, but staying far enough ahead of Heishi and Tiane to allow for some privacy.

"So, you saw Aldith burn in?" Heishi asked after they had walked in silence for some time.

"Roger that, Top. I could be wrong, but her chute wasn't deployed, and I saw her bounce. That narrows down possible outcomes in my opinion..."

"When we return to Terminus, we will take time to mourn for our newest team member, but for now we cannot focus on such things. What a waste, though, she seemed to be a decent fit with our team."

"Top, I have to ask: do you think we will ever get home again?" Tiane had a look on his face that was difficult to read as he asked.

"Well, I honestly don't know my brother. I still have no idea where that storm came from, or how we were sent here. I suppose if there is a way to predict these shifts in the planes of existence then we could go through another one, but there is no way to know where we would end up. We really need to find Zatus. If anyone can figure this out, he can." Heishi looked Tiane in the face as he spoke, trying to judge the reaction his words would have on the young sniper.

"I have had over three months to think about it. I don't see what the difference is whether we stay here or go back. I have no family there, other than you and the guys, and now that I found you and know there is civilization here, I say we explore and see what this world has to offer. Besides, if what you say is true that we might be able to predict a shift and go through it, who is to say we don't end up somewhere worse than this place?" Tiane stared at the ground as he spoke, as if he was ashamed to even consider not going back to his own world.

"You have an excellent point. If we can find a way to do some good here, we should. But let's call staying here Plan B for now and see if going back is even an option. I must admit, though, that living in a fantasy novel sounds a bit appealing. Let's just hope we don't get eaten by a dragon," Heishi laughed, which did much to lighten the mood between the two.

As they walked and talked about the possibilities before them, dark clouds began to gather above the group. The day had been rather pleasant, but the further they walked the more the wind picked up, blowing against them and making it difficult to continue. As the path narrowed further and began to climb the side of the mountain, rain began to dump on them, making it dangerous to continue.

"Is this type of storm normal for this region?" Heishi asked the party members.

"Do you want more lightning, little man?" Yutri laughed, and Shenroc slapped him in the back of the head. "It is just a joke, my friend. Yes, these storms are common this time of year. Usually I find a room with a fire and stay there, but it appears we shall stay out and get wet today! If we are lucky, it will only last a short time, but it could go on for a day or more."

"We should make a shelter under the trees and see what this storm will do," Di'eslo recommended as he looked at the sky. "I saw a clearing a little way back," he shouted to be heard above the wind.

Agreeing with his assessment, the party

moved back down the path until the clearing came into view. As they closed in on the objective, the ground became continually slicker as the torrential downpour turned the ground the consistency of soup. As Tiane lead them into the clearing and found an outcropping of rocks to break the rain, a growl rumbled across the empty space. As the humans watched, a monster burst from the trees to the right of Yutri, knocking Shenroc to the side and pinning the dwarf beneath a pile of wet fur and muscle. Yutri yelped with surprise, struggling to keep teeth the size of his fist from ripping into the exposed flesh of his neck.

Leaping into action, Di'eslo rushed the beast, leading with his shield to protect him from the six legs, each ending with razor sharp claws that ripped at Yutri. If not for his mithril armor, the dwarf would have been shredded in the initial assault, but Dwarvish armor would not fail so easily. Di'eslo whispered a word under his breath, and a web launched from his shield, glowing purple and wrapping two of the legs together, immobilizing them. He swung his flail with abandon, each strike sparking with power as the spikes glowed brighter and brighter each time it connected with the beast.

The beast rolled to the side and kicked out with a free leg, smacking Di'eslo in the chest and sending him sliding in the muck. Shenroc could not gain footing to use his claymore with any weight behind the swing, so he let out a bestial roar as he charged in with his twin daggers. He immediately scored several hits, and blue blood began to flow freely from the beast. The head snapped his direction, two rows of five eyes each focusing on the half-orc, and razor-sharp teeth closed on his left arm. It began shaking side to side, grinding into the armor his forearm. The mithril held, but a sickening crunching sound emerged as his bones popped under the powerful jaws.

A trio of throwing knives flew past his head as he tried to break free of the beast, each sticking into a different eye. It screamed, releasing Shenroc from its grasp, and turned fully toward Heishi as he followed the flying blades with his katana, green lightning flashing as he swung and cut off one of the legs that had Yutri pinned. Di'eslo held his shield forth, his eyes glowing a brilliant shade of blue as he focused on Shenroc and a wave of healing energy engulfed the half-orc, knitting bone back together as he focused. Yutri, now released from the bulk of the beast, stood and began a battle song as he repeatedly pounded his war hammer against the head.

Realizing it was outmatched, the beast, which resembled a grey six-legged tiger, attempted to disengage. It was able to push back a few paces, but two legs were still ensnared in the web Di'eslo threw from his shield and a third leg had been removed by Heishi, so the movement was too slow. Tiane, not to be left out of the melee, too a few strides, used Yutri's now raised shield to spring from, and landed on the back of the beast, green flames flaring as he hacked into the beast with his kamas. The beast rolled on its back and attempted to swipe the maniac, but all that accomplished was to give Tiane a clear path to its neck, where he buried a kama blade fully. The remaining seven eyes opened wide as the beast realized it was about to die, and Tiane pulled his blade to the side, ripping the head half off. Panting, he rose from the mud and blood as the beast stopped moving.

"Those are easier to kill with a .308 round to the head," Tiane muttered as he stumbled away from the corpse.

"What was that?" breathed Heishi, clearly rattled by the sudden appearance of the prowling nightmare, now dead before him.

"The orcs call them 'ekastatu,' although I have never met a human who has seen one and lived to tell the tale. They prowl the mountain regions, where they rule as the top predators. We are lucky to have such powerful companions," Shenroc nodded to Di'eslo as he spoke, "especially one who could save my arm.

Let us take shelter from the storm before anything else decides Yutri looks like a meal."

The outcropping of rocks turned out to be a cave, which went deeper into the mountain than the group thought it would. The companions struggled to bring in wood from the surrounding trees, now wet from the rain, and Tiane used a chemical compound created by Zatus to start a fire. The chemicals burned hotter than white phosphorous, drying the wood almost instantly and within minutes the group had a fire to begin drying their gear while they ate a small meal.

"Amazing, I have never seen wet wood catch fire so quickly," Shenroc commented as he slid his feet a bit closer to the blaze to warm them.

"If we can find our other two lost companions you will see even more wondrous things than that," Heishi grinned.

"This must be where the ekastatu was headed when it found us," Di'eslo commented, looking around the cave. "I found some old bones deeper in the cave, it would make sense that the beast called this place a home. I would suggest vigilance while we weather the storm, it would not do to be surprised by another such beast in these close quarters."

Agreeing with his assessment, the companions decided to leave a guard and let the others rest while it was possible. "I'll take the first shift," stated Heishi, "the rest of you seem to have an easier time seeing at night than I do, and it will be dark soon. Which reminds me, how was Tiane able to attune to the darkness and I have not?"

Di'eslo took a few moments, poking the fire with a stick, then answered, "The Art comes differently to everyone. In my experience, we all can interact with the energy surrounding us, though most never take the time to learn. Call it 'natural talent,' if you will, but the gifts we discover relate to the person. If you are naturally able to swim well, you may find yourself able to hold your breath for longer periods than should be possible. In the case of Tiane, he must be naturally comfortable in the dark, and as he focused his senses became sharpened inadvertently because of it. If you take time to focus, you too may find a gift you were previously unaware of."

Confused, Yutri asked, "Is that why the ladies love me so much?"

"No, you oaf, that is just your delusions deceiving you," Shenroc laughed.

The conversation gradually declined, and the companions each drifted off to sleep as Heishi stood watch over them. Pondering what Di'eslo had explained, he spent some time focusing on his surroundings, trying to feel the energy that surrounded him. He passed his time trying to feel the rain, trying to see the wind, and nothing came of it. Frustrated, he woke Yutri for his watch and drifted off to sleep.

The night passed uneventfully, and early the next morning the rain stopped as the sun was rising. The group ate a small meal as the sun came fully into the sky, beginning to dry the mud caused by the deluge of the previous day. When the meal was finished, Heishi consulted the map, and they once again began the trek to the orc cave. There was less talking this day, as the surprise attack had them each on edge, and their pace quickened with expectation of getting out of the woods.

After noon had passed, they came around the edge of the mountain and saw a lake below them while the path wound higher up the mountain. "This has to be it," Heishi stated. "The map says there is an entrance toward the peak of the mountain and another down in those trees next to the lake. So, the question is, which should we take?"

"I have dealt with many orcs before I left my people," Di'eslo began. "I lived deep under the surface, where the light is never seen, and we used orcs and goblins as slaves. From all I know of their kind, they like to come out at higher elevations when they raid the surface, as it gives the advantage of high ground if they must fight their way out. My guess is the lower entrance will be guarded mostly by goblins or other fodder races to give the orcs advanced warning of intruders while the upper entrance will be guarded by orc warriors. Shenroc, what say you?"

Sheepishly, Shenroc looked at the ground as he answered, "I do not know much of orc tactics. My mother was not exactly what one would call a 'willing participant' in my conception. When I was younger, I attempted to learn more of my orc heritage, especially when the human children began to bully me because of it. Orcs are less kind to half-breeds than humans are, so I chose to live in Terminus, where even a half-orc can find his way if he is not opposed to moral grey areas."

It was clear Shenroc was uncomfortable speaking of his past, so Di'eslo stepped in to save him. "Well, it would appear I have the best understanding of our enemies then. Is it agreed we enter through the lower cave?"

Chapter 9 – The Caves

The companions made their way as stealthily as possible to the bottom of the mountain, always angling for the trees that separated it from the lake. Di'eslo had assured the group that goblinkin were sensitive to sunlight and that they should be relatively safe outside the caves during the day, but no one was willing to trust too fully in that assurance. As they closed in on the targeted group of trees, they slowed their pace considerably, not wanting to be surprised by any animals that might make the area their home.

Their caution turned out to be unnecessary, and in a short time they discovered the entrance to the caves. It was a smaller opening than would be expected. It appeared to be nothing more than a small cave rather than the entrance to an extensive underground network of larger caves and caverns. Scattered around the mouth of the cave were the bones of small animals and other such garbage, which Di'eslo quietly communicated was evidence of goblins in the area. The sun was still overhead, so there was no movement outside the cave, but the stench carried up to the group on the breeze was all the evidence needed to determine they were in the correct location.

Di'eslo lead the group toward the cave, taking advantage of as much cover as possible, but hoping the goblins would be less on their guard if they saw a shadow elf approaching, with Shenroc close behind him for the same reason. The rest stayed low, which was no small feat for Yutri, and followed as cautiously as possible. As they approached the last boulder before the open area in front of the cave, the group stopped.

"Shenroc and I will go first," Di'eslo whispered to his companions. "Hopefully the sun behind us will distort their vision enough that they will not recognize his human blood. When we enter the cave, watch for either an all clear signal," he waved his hand and gave a thumbs up signal, "or listen for the fight. Either way, make your way into the cave as quickly as possible: do not stand in the open for longer than you must, as there should be more lookout positions hidden in the rocks above."

Interesting, a thumbs up is a universal "all clear" signal in more than just our world. I wonder if giving the bird means the same thing here...

"Heishi, are you listening to me?" Di'eslo was staring right at him.

"Roger, I got you covered," Heishi

responded quickly.

"Who is Roger?" inquired Di'eslo, scrunching up his face in confusion.

"He's friends with some guy named Will that everyone wants to fire at," replied Tiane with a grin.

"It is how Soldiers acknowledge messages are received and understood. I apologize, I will attempt to avoid such slang in the future," Heishi answered, shooting Tiane a glare as he did.

Di'eslo nodded his understanding, then stood and walked boldly into the center of the clearing. He looked around with a haughty expression, then snapped his fingers as if beckoning a slave, and Shenroc obediently followed, head hung and giving the appearance of utter brokenness. Di'eslo waited for him to catch up, then slapped him across the face, adding in broken orcish, *"If I must wait for you again, slave, I will feed you to the ekastatu."*

"Me sorry, great one. I no do again," Shenroc replied, hoping his orcish was acceptable after so many years of avoiding the tongue of his paternal heritage.

Di'eslo sneered, slapped him again, then turned and strode boldly into the mouth of the cave, the shadows curling every direction from his skin as the sunlight shone on it. Inside the cave, he took a moment to shift his vision to see in the dark, and as it adjusted, he was taken slightly aback by four goblin forms standing in the darkness, pointing spears at him. Playing the part of the superior shadow elf, he swung his shield from his back as he jerked his flail from his side in one fluid motion, never taking his sight from the goblins.

"How dare you point those sticks at me, worthless slaves," Di'eslo snarled at them, taking a few steps forward and swinging his flail a few times for good measure. Shenroc advanced behind him, easing his daggers from his hips, as the cave was too tight for a mighty claymore.

"We no slaves of you, we's serve the mighty Sgel," the goblins retorted, attempting to appear as if they were not frightened at the sudden appearance of a shadow elf noble and his orc slave.

Hoping to gain information about the orc leader, where to find him, and whether he held the orb they were sent to acquire, Di'eslo took one more step and stopped to stare at the goblins, just barely three steps away from him. Without warning, he swung his flail and smashed the speaker in the head, burying it in the skull of the pitiful thing.

"You will speak when spoken to, and only to answer questions, or I will kill all of you. Do you understand me, rodents?"

The other three dropped their spears

immediately and prostrated themselves on the floor in front of the mighty shadow elf. Di'eslo nodded to Shenroc, who proceeded to give the "thumbs up" signal from the mouth of the cave, setting the rest of the group in motion. He then looked down on the groveling minions before him and began his interrogation.

"Who is this Sgel you serve?"

"He the master of all. Sgel the Nasty. He kill everyone and rule world," the next goblin in line stuttered, face still in the dirt.

Di'eslo swung his flail and bashed that one in the head, the pool of black blood from the two dead goblins beginning to spread across the floor of the cave. *"Wrong. This Sgel the Nasty will bow to me. Tell me the correct answer, slave, or you will be next. Where can I find this Sgel the Nasty?"*

"He find you, you no find hi--" the third goblin began, before his head, too was caved in. The spikes of the flail Di'eslo swung expertly glowing brighter with each attack.

"Last chance to live, slave. Where is this Sgel the Nasty?" Di'eslo threatened the final goblin guard.

"He deep in mountain. Him throne in big cave. One way in, no way out," the goblin risked a look up at the shadow elf as he spoke, and a yelp escaped his lips as he saw the Dwarf and Human enter the cave, smiling at the two in front of him. *"What this? You no elf lord, you are*

traitor!" it screamed, reaching for the sharpened stick it used as a spear.

"Wrong answer," Di'eslo stated, reverting to the common tongue as he swung his flail a last time. As the flail connected with the skull of the goblin, he released the building energy in the spikes, causing a small explosion that ripped the head clean off and sent it flying across the cave. Stunned silence followed the strike, with all eyes on Di'eslo and his flail. Turning to his companions with a grin, he simply stated, "Not all weapons are created equal. It is good to know the Art," then turned and began moving silently toward the tunnel in the rear of the cave.

The tunnel was approximately five feet wide, with a ceiling that started just above Yutri's head and sloped upward the further down they traveled until it was lost from view in the darkness. Heishi stayed in the middle of the group as the light faded, as he was the only member of the group unable to see in the darkness. Occasionally there were cracks in the stone where light shone through dimly, giving just enough light for him to not stumble on the rough floor, but for the most part he was blind.

"You ok, Top?" Tiane asked as the tunnel smoothed out a bit and the cracks in the rock became less common.

"Getting harder to see is all. If we ever get to a point where stealth is not the key, I'll set fire to something. Too bad we weren't headed out for a night mission, right?" Heishi smiled in the darkness, unsure of whether Tiane could see facial expressions with his new ability or not. "I keep trying what you did to feel the darkness and I get nothing. My senses are heightened here compared to home, but no matter what I try I am still running blind here."

Hearing the conversation, Di'eslo whispered a word and the web on his shield brightened a bit, casting a purple glow around the group. "I am sorry, my friend, I sometimes forget not everyone can see in the darkness. This should help and will not give away our location."

"You are full of surprises. Thank you, that does help," Heishi replied.

The tunnel continued deeper into the mountain, and soon they were halted by Shenroc, who was now in the lead to keep the light of the shield in the rear. "Around this bend the tunnel opens into a cavern. I have not been able to see far into it yet, but I can see it widening inside. How should we proceed?"

Di'eslo doused the light from his shield as he replied, "I will go first and see what is there." He slipped ahead of the group, calling upon the darkness to shroud his appearance. By his fourth step in front of the group, even Tiane could not see his heat signature as he moved through the inky blackness of the cave. He returned after a short time, appearing suddenly from the darkness and making the group jump a bit in surprise.

"It is an empty cavern, although I admit I cannot see the ceiling. There are three tunnels that continue, two on the left side, and one in the back-right corner. From the air currents I could feel, the tunnel on the right leads deeper underground, the first on the left had no air flow which usually implies another cavern past it, and the far-left leads upward. The goblin said Sgel is deep under the mountain; I would recommend the path to the right."

The group agreed, and Shenroc and Yutri lead the way into the cavern. Deciding to err on the side of caution, Di'eslo and Tiane stayed to the left and right of Heishi, walking him through the darkness rather than lighting the shield again. Halfway around the edge of the cave, a primal roar broke the silence followed by a screeching sound from above.

"Galad!" Di'eslo shouted, and his shield blazed with a purple light that immediately stole the darkness.

Swooping toward them from above, the companions saw three giant bats with orcs riding on their backs. The bats wore crude armor that covered their torso, and the orcs wielded spears and wore a mixture of chain and leather armor, with spikes protruding from the shoulders. They wore helmets with horns that protruded from both sides, and they screamed war cries as the bats descended on the intruders. Di'eslo angled his shield toward the attackers, half-closed his eyes, and whispered, *"Dain,"* creating an area of silence around the beasts as they swooped in, the first orc jabbing at him and connecting solidly with his shield. The impact rocked the elf back on his heels, but the silence held, containing all sound. The bat beat its wings and moved out of range as Di'eslo swung his flail in response, just catching one of its legs and disrupting its balance. The beast hovered in mid-air above him for a moment as it angled for another attack, its orc rider clearly screaming but unable to produce any sound.

Heishi, excited to finally be able to see, smoothly pulled his katana from the saya, igniting the green electricity inherent to the blade as he brought it into a defensive position in front of him. Purple and green shadows bounced around the walls of the cavern as the second bat flew toward the new source of light. It proved to be a fatal mistake, as the crude armoring the bat wore could not protect it from his blade. As the bat closed, mouth coming in a shriek of anger, Heishi dropped to his knees, slashing the bottom jaw from the beast and continuing the cut down its midsection, spraying intestines and blood across the floor as it crashed into the wall, quite dead.

The orc rider leaped clear of the wall before his mount crashed into it, putting himself into a clumsy but effective roll as he landed to absorb some of the impact. He swung around and hurled the spear at Heishi, who deftly picked it out of the air with the side of his blade, deflecting it harmlessly away from the group. The orc, as the spear flew towards his prey, pulled a club with spikes stuck through the head of it from next to his saddle on the bat, and charged Heishi, his face a mask of fury. He only made it a few steps before he stopped in mid-run, a thrown mithril war hammer smashing into his chest and crumpling him to the floor. Heishi looked toward Yutri, who rushed the orc, mouth open and clearly singing a battle song in the silence. He retrieved his hammer, turned to toss Heishi a wink, then spun and slammed it into the skull of the shattered orc.

The third bat rider, seeing Di'eslo squared off with the first, came around his back side, attempting to take out the dangerous elf. The bat was poised to swoop in for the kill, when a flash of light appeared from the right and it suddenly jerked to the left, falling twenty feet to the ground, quite dead. As the shocked orc crashed to the floor, it had only a moment to look around the cavern for the source of the attack. He made eye contact with Tiane just as he dropped his rifle, ignited the green flames of his kamas, and threw his right-hand weapon. Running toward the orc as the kama spun through the air, he closed the distance a moment after the blade struck the orc, digging into its shoulder and continuing to burn. The shocked orc yanked free the kama, which immediately doused the flame, and swung it at the puny human rushing toward him. Tiane slid under the swipe of his weapon, causing the blade to retract into the handle with a thought, and buried his second blade into the stomach of his opponent. A confused expression passed over the face of the doomed orc as it stared at the seemingly harmless wooden handle he now held. He turned it toward his face, and Tiane caused the blade to spring back from the handle, igniting the flame and watching it bury itself in the orc's face. Grinning at the stupidity of the creature, he wrenched both blades free and turned back to the general melee around him.

The first bat rider, seeing his companions die swiftly and easily, attempted to break contact with Di'eslo and return to the safety of the darkness above. Not out of tricks yet, Di'eslo used his shield to launch a glowing purple web at the bat, which stuck the left wing to its body, causing it to fall to the floor, alive but stunned. The orc rider leapt from the back of the crumpled bat, retrieving a two-handed axe from the saddle of the bat.

Shenroc dashed in, his claymore flashing in the artificial lights produced by his companions. The larger orc blocked his first swing, redirecting the weight of the blow to its left as it stepped to the right. No novice to battle, Shenroc recovered from the wild swing and turned toward his opponent, stopping the swing of its axe with his own blade. As he held the axe in place, struggling against the superior strength of the full-blooded orc, he kicked out with his right leg, connecting solidly with his opponent's kneecap and shattering it. The orc stumbled back, silently howling in pain, and dropped to its good knee. Expecting the trap, Shenroc came on in a fury anyway, an overhead swing of his claymore aimed directly for the orc skull. Before the orc could respond, he released the blade, allowing it to be batted harmlessly aside by the orc's axe, pulling both daggers from his sides and burying them in either side of the orc's neck. He stared his opponent in the eyes as the realization that a half-breed had just killed him, then ripped both blades free as he kicked the orc in the chest, the serrations tearing chunks from its flesh and the body dropping harmlessly to the floor. He returned his blades to their sheathes, retrieved his claymore, and turned back to the main group, prepared for more bloodshed.

As Shenroc battled the orc, Di'eslo smiled, slowly walking toward the bat. He spun the ball of his flail around as he walked, staring the beast in the eye as it attempted to break free of the web. As he came in range, the bat swiped at him with a free claw, which he batted to the side with his shield, then buried the flail in the skull of the bat. Sighing, he turned to see the fight was over, and removed his silence from the area.

"You are full of surprises, elf. Glad you are on our side," Heishi exclaimed as he realized he could speak and be heard. "What was that?"

"A simple ability I learned to cover an area in complete silence. I typically use it to cover the cries of the wounded until I can assist them: it is discomforting to other wounded Soldiers to hear the screams of their companions. In this case, I assumed we still wanted stealth on our side. I can only hope I enacted the silence before others heard the cries of these two," he finished, kicking the bat he had just dispatched. "I still am enchanted by these weapons you and your friend carry which kill from such distances. An arrow from a long bow would have had difficulty reaching that bat from where Tiane was kneeling and would not have killed it with a single shot." He looked expectantly at Heishi, waiting for a response as Shenroc and Yutri crowded him, also wanting to learn the source of this power.

"They are called 'guns,' and are the weapon of choice in our world. We only train with martial weapons as a discipline, we happened to have them this time because of the nature of the mission we were carrying out." He removed a magazine from its pouch on his belt and removed a bullet from the magazine. "This is a bullet. Inside the casing is a black powder that burns at a high temperature, and when compressed it will cause an explosion. The explosion from the powder propels the projectile from the front of the round, and if it is encased in a gun the barrel of the gun will direct the projectile. The problem we will have here is that when we run out of bullets, our guns will be useless, which is why I have only used my pistol once since I arrived here. Tiane is what we call a 'sniper,' and is a master at remaining hidden for days at a time to take a single shot to kill his intended target. As far as I am aware, he does not miss. Ever. His rifle carries more power than my pistol, and that is why he uses it from long distances to kill quickly and efficiently. You would be amazed how far that the kid can shoot." As he finished explaining, the other three nodded in appreciation.

"Is there a way to make more of these bullets here in our world?" Shenroc inquired.

"If we can find the right components it

would not be difficult. When we have some time, Tiane and I can search for the right components to make the black powder. If we can do that, we can reload the brass casings of the bullets. Creating the casings would be quite an intricate procedure, and I am not sure we would be able to do that here," Heishi answered.

"Dwarves can build anything," Yutri stated as he puffed up his chest with pride. He leaned over to Shenroc and whispered, "What is this 'intricate'?" then blushed as he realized everyone heard his question.

"Intricate means too tiny for your hands, you oaf," Shenroc stated as he attempted to keep a straight face.

"Dwarves can build anything, but that is pretty small. We may be able to hire a gnome to put it together if you can find the components required," Di'eslo responded, smiling at the dwarf.

As they discussed the possibility of manufacturing more bullets, Tiane returned with his rifle slung across his back again. Grinning sheepishly at being the center of attention, he stepped to the side of Heishi and waited patiently for the conversation to end.

"Let us continue before anyone discovers this mess. We have been lucky so far, but I fear it will get very bloody very soon," Heishi said, gesturing to Shenroc to again take the lead.

Di'eslo dimmed the light of his shield and waited for Shenroc to lead them to the tunnel on the right before proceeding. As they walked across the remainder of the cavern, Heishi asked, "What were you yelling at the beginning of the fight?"

"'*Galad*' is the elvish word for 'light,' and '*dain*' is elvish for 'silence.' As I explained, there are no 'magic words' or 'incantations' necessary for the Art, however, some of the more difficult abilities I have learned take more focus than others. In the heat of battle, I often revert to the elvish tongue and speak the words to help me focus on what I want to accomplish, and it has served me well."

Heishi walked in silence for a few paces, then nodded. "Do you think that could help me learn how to use the Art?"

"It cannot hurt, my friend. But do not rush, it may take some time for you to discover what you are capable of. Many are never able to at all, so do not be discouraged. Just be patient and learn what you may," Di'eslo replied with a sense of finality. "Now we must be silent, sound carries long distances down here. If we are lucky the initial battle cries will echo so no stupid orcs are able to follow the sound. But in the depths, orcs and goblins are the least of our concerns. Let us hope nothing hungry comes looking for us..."

Chapter 10 – The Nasty

For several uneventful hours, Shenroc lead the team through twisting and turning tunnels in the dark. The tunnels were wide and the ceiling high, so they remained on guard for more bat riders, but their caution seemed unnecessary. As they traveled, it became more and more difficult to remain vigilant, and each member began to wonder if they were on a wild goose chase. After clearing yet another cavern uneventfully, Shenroc signaled the group to come in close.

"I will stop here to take a rest," he began, looking at each man for confirmation of his plan "There is only the one entrance and one exit to this cavern, so we can alternately stand guard and rest a while. This could still take some time, as I have seen plenty of evidence of goblins or orcs but do not know where they may be."

"We are headed in the right direction, the stench of goblinkin grows the deeper we descend. If we do not find them soon, I will be surprised," Di'eslo confirmed, then moved forward to the exit tunnel to stand guard, dousing the light from his shield as he moved.

Shenroc volunteered to take the first rear

guard shift, and silently crept back the way they had come, leaving the other three to eat a quick meal.

Sitting in darkness, the silence of the cavern pressed in on the companions. As Heishi sat eating a loaf of bread and some rat meat he had acquired from The Portal; he felt a slight vibration in the stone. Unsure if that was possible, he paused, stopped chewing, and waited. A few heartbeats later, he felt the vibration again, and it was stronger this second time. When he felt a third vibration, he pulled Tiane close so he could whisper in his ear and explained what he was feeling.

"Top," he whispered back, "I don't feel anything."

"It is definitely getting stronger and more consistent, almost like footsteps, but heavy enough to shake the ground. Are you keeping visual contact with our sentries?"

"I can see everything, they are both at the edges of the tunnels," Tiane replied, looking from Di'eslo to Shenroc in turn.

"Go relieve Di'eslo and send him this way. He is more in tune with the darkness and tunnels than Shenroc is. If I could see anything without his shield, I would have had him on point this whole time. Quickly and quietly get him back here, the vibrations are getting stronger," Heishi ordered, attempting to keep the worry out of his voice.

Tiane slipped away, relieving Di'eslo at his post and sending him back to Heishi. As he slid to the floor next to his new friend, Di'eslo whispered "galad," and his shield glowed dimly. "What is the matter?"

"You will want to extinguish that light. Something is coming toward us: something big. I can feel vibrations in the stone; they were faint at first, but are getting stronger as I sit here," Heishi replied in a hushed tone.

Looking at Yutri, Di'eslo gave the dwarf a questioning look. "Dwarves are more in tune with rock than most races, have you felt anything, my large friend?"

"I am embarrassed to admit I feel nothi-" he broke off in mid-sentence, his face screwing up momentarily. "Yes, there it is. It is faint, but there is a rhythm to it. It is not something large, it feels like an army marching." He paused for a few more moments, then smiled, "Do not worry, my friends, it is above us."

"How can you be certain," Heishi inquired. "I can feel the vibrations in the stone and can tell now that it is a large group marching mostly in step with each other, but I cannot tell the distance or direction."

"A dwarf knows what a dwarf knows, human," Yutri stifled a laugh. "If you live a few centuries, you too will be able to tell."

Accepting that answer, Heishi nodded and turned to Di'eslo. "What do we do? Are we in the wrong location? I have no desire to run into an army down here, as I do not even know where 'down here' is anymore."

"We are still going the right way, my friend. If the smell in the air signifies anything, I have a feeling we will find this cavern of Sgel shortly after our break. Ensure you eat, I do not know when we will be able to again." With that, Di'eslo winked a red eye at Heishi and stepped into a shadow, disappearing immediately and extinguishing the light simultaneously.

Having enough of the dark, Heishi slid his katana from its saya, placing it on the rock next to his leg and activating the blade. The green electricity sparked up and down the blade, casting ominous shadows around the cavern, but it was better than the pitch black he had been unable to grow accustomed to. He ate quickly as Tiane returned, having been relieved by Di'eslo, then asked Yutri to relieve Shenroc. "The sooner we find this Sgel, the sooner we get back to sunshine and fresh air."

"And rain and ekastatu," muttered Yutri as he moved away to relieve Shenroc.

"Is it just me, or does he seem to like it better down here in this hole?" Heishi asked, looking at his friend.

"What do I know, other than watching

some movies and reading books about dwarves and elves when I was a kid," responded Tiane.

"Fair enough. Make sure you eat something, these vibrations in the rock above us are making me nervous and I am ready to be done with this place."

After each member of the group had finished eating, Shenroc lead them into the next tunnel. This one was different, as it narrowed considerably as they moved along, and the stench of rotting meat and unwashed bodies became evident to the entire party. A short time later, the winding tunnel came to an end at the top of a stairway leading down. The steps were roughhewn stone, but it was obvious a crude stoneworker had made the steps purposely.

"It would appear we are close to the throne room of Sgel. We are vulnerable on the stairs, move quickly and quietly, but be cautious," Di'eslo advised. "Heishi, you should use your sword for light again, I will lead us down the stairs, cloaked in shadow. Shenroc will come behind me, Yutri in the rear as he is the least stealthy of us...even without a need for a light." He smiled at Yutri, who did not appear to understand the joke at his expense, then doused the light of his shield as Heishi activated his blade. When the party was set again, he stepped forward and allowed the shadows to embrace him, obscuring him from sight entirely when he was not moving, even in the light of the sword.

Creeping down the stairs, the companions maintained a heightened sense of awareness, but it was unnecessary as the stairway was empty, ending in front of a massive stone door. Yutri made his way to the door and spent some time checking for traps, as Shenroc quietly explained to the humans that Dwarves could find flaws in any construction, which is where a trap would be hidden, thus making them experts at finding them.

"The problem is when the oaf tries to disarm traps," Shenroc explained, putting his hands together at the fingertips, then spreading them out, mimicking an explosion.

"The good news, my funny friend," Yutri started, "Is there are no traps." He paused for a few moments, building the suspense and clearly enjoying the attention. "The bad news is there is no way to open this door. If the tunnel was worked properly, I would guess a dwarf king had this door built, but an orc? I do not understand how this door is here, but it will not open."

"Let one of us have a look if you are sure there are no traps," Shenroc said as he moved toward the door. "You remember the last time you tried to solve a puzzle? I almost died fighting guards while you tried to figure out to write 'six' on the tablet to open the door."

Stifling a laugh, the four remaining members of the group began to scour the face of the door, searching for any possible way to open it. Concluding there was no mechanism to open it, Yutri grinned in triumph at the other four. "You are not so smart now, are you? Would you like to see a trick to open this?" Before another word could be spoken, he lifted his massive war hammer and smashed it into the door three times in quick succession.

"WHAT. ARE. YOU. DOING?" Shenroc annunciated every syllable as he stared at Yutri.

"Opening the door," he replied, looking rather proud of himself.

"That did not open the door..." Shenroc began, then stopped as the door silently slid upward, revealing a large cavern lit by torches beyond.

"Come in here, trespassers, and let me see you," boomed a voice from the other side of the cavern. The voice was deep, spoken in the common tongue, and without the broken language typically associated with orcs.

Cautiously, Di'eslo stepped through the door, his shield in front of him and his other hand on his flail for ease of access. Behind him followed Yutri, also keeping his shield ahead of himself, war hammer still in hand, and still grinning at his own cleverness. Heishi deactivated his blade and slid it back in the saya, not wanting to start a fight unless it was necessary, then followed Yutri through the door. Tiane and Shenroc brought up the rear, both walking cautiously, and as they passed through the door it slid noiselessly back into place behind them.

The cavern was the largest they had yet encountered, at least 300M long, with stone pillars running down the center, creating a walkway to approach the throne in the center. The pillars were built with the same craftsmanship as the door and were out of place in the throne room of an orc king, as were the straight walls engraved with what appeared to be hieroglyphics of ancient battles. Orc and goblin guards milled around the outside of the pillars in mismatched armor, holding rusty weapons, and attempting to look important.

As they approached the throne, they got their first look at the dirtiest orc any of them had ever laid eyes on. Sgel the Nasty was appropriately named, and the smell that assaulted the senses of the companions brought tears to even Shenroc's eyes. He sat on a throne covered in animal skins that clearly had not been tanned properly, as the rotting smell emanating from the throne was unbearable. As they approached, he stood up to his full seven-foot height, expecting his massive bulk intimidate all in the room. His guards cowered before their king, with scalps of every imaginable race living on Kartos hanging from his belt. He wore no shirt, preferring to let his fat stomach hang out over the loincloth he wore as his only covering. Dirt and dried blood covered every visible inch of his body, both his skin and the little clothing he wore. A gigantic tusk protruded from the left side of his mouth, and a second broken tusk hung loosely from the right side.

"I know what you have come for, and you cannot have it," Sgel stated smugly as he held out the orb in his left hand. It appeared black in color, with a constant swirl of red making its way around the interior of the orb. The black of the orb was dark, absorbing the light of the torches around the throne, but the red swirls glowed with an internal iridescent quality. "It is mine and will continue to be so."

Taken slightly aback by his speech and willingness to present the prize they sought; the companions could do nothing but look at each other with confusion. "Why would you allow us access to your throne room if you knew what we came to retrieve?" a stunned Heishi asked.

"You are strong, this I have seen. Yes, human, I have watched the five of you ever since you entered my domain. But you cannot match the power I hold in my hand any more than the one who sent you could. Make no mistake, if you do not leave with a message for Puny Jim to never enter my home again, I will kill you all and send the pieces back to him in a box. This I have seen," Sgel grinned smugly as he replied, drool hanging from the edge of his broken tusk.

"If I may ask, mighty one, what is this orb, and why does Jim want it so badly?" Heishi asked, feigning subservience and averting his eyes.

"Ahh, yes, the smooth-talking leader of the other-worlders. Yes, I have seen you, the one they call Heishi. You may feel free to stop the act; I have been watching you and your companion since you arrived. I am Sgel the Nasty, and I know all and see all!" he stated, flatulating loudly as he completed his exclamation.

Raising his gaze to look the orc in the eyes again, Heishi nodded once and grinned. "Fair enough, Sgel the Nasty. But my question remains, what is this orb and why did Jim send us to take it from you? He simply said it was stolen from him by orcs and to retrieve it for him. I did not expect to hold a civil conversation with the orc king and would very much like some answers as I do not appreciate being played like a fool."

A tense moment passed as Sgel stared at the human before him, then he let out a deep laugh before answering. "The orb is one of many items of power in this world. Where did it come from? I do not know. What I do know is that when I took possession of it, my mind was opened to the secrets of Kartos. Nothing is hidden from my sight, and I will not give it up. For too long, you humans and elves have ruled this world, looking down on what you consider *'lesser races,'* but that day has ended. Maybe you heard my army marching forth to conquer as you descended to my halls. So be it. There is nothing you or any other human can do to stop the destruction that is coming to your world, and when it is turned to ash, it will be remade to my desire. Go now, tell Puny Jim what I have told you, and let him know that my orb is protected in this throne room! None may enter unless I allow it, and none may leave without my blessing."

As Sgel continued his monologue, full of himself and not giving credit to the warrior before him, Heishi inched closer to the throne and the wind bag standing before it. So confident was the orc king in his own power that he was not even looking at Heishi as he spoke, he was looking into a large mirror positioned on the closest pillar to the throne. As he crept slowly forward, Heishi tried to feel the room around him. He could feel the air currents, and as he focused, he felt the world around him slow down as he continued to move.

Faster than any in the room had ever seen, his right hand slipped across his body, pulling the first throwing dagger and releasing it before any eye registered the movement. Sgel continued his boasting, unaware of the danger until the first dagger pierced him in the hand, forcing him to drop the orb to the floor. His surprise was complete as the second and third daggers pierced his throat and left eye split seconds apart. Before the gurgle of air mixed with blood could be heard, Heishi had already slid his katana from its saya and leapt forward, igniting the power in the blade and swiping across, beheading the filthy orc king. He spun back on the room as the head of Sgel the Nasty fell from his shoulders and his throwing daggers reappeared on his wrist, prepared to defend against retaliation, but a stunned silence held in the cavern.

"That's one way to do it, Top," Tiane breathed. "I've never seen anyone move so fast."

With the silence broken, the companions rushed the throne, taking up defensive positions around Heishi and the orb. The guards of Sgel stood with mouths gaping at the intruder who had dispatched their god-king so quickly and easily. For a few moments there was a standoff, with the guards staring at the intruders surrounding the corpse of their king and the companions waiting anxiously for the response of the guards.

With a primal scream, the first guard took the first step toward the throne, huge battle axe raised above his head. He was instantly stopped, the fletching of an arrow protruding from his eye socket as Tiane smoothly slid another arrow from his quiver and to his bow with a sly grin. That was all the rest of the guards needed to be urged into action. The larger orcs commanded the goblins to rush the throne and avenge Sgel the Nasty, while they waited behind the swarm of goblin fodder. In a blink, a score of goblins appeared from all sides of the room, attempting to take the powerful companions down in a horde of flailing clubs and spears.

Arrows rained on the first wave of the beasts, Tiane grinning and taunting as he fired. "Little guy, you'll have to do better than that! Ohh, that one didn't even make it five steps! Hey, Top, how many have you got so far?" Tiane laughed maniacally as he unleashed death on the monsters rushing toward him.

As they came, Heishi threw his daggers repeatedly, instantly recalling them to himself as they connected with his targets. Goblin blood flowed like a river before the throne as the beasts were whipped into a frenzy at the audacity of these intruders to attack their king.

Di'eslo and Yutri stood side by side in front of the rest creating a shield wall to protect their companions from the arrows and spears flying toward them as the goblins charged. Yutri sang a Dwarvish battle song, laughing and reveling in the carnage before him.

"Hey now, do not kill them all, I want a turn too!" Yutri cried, a feigned look of sadness on his face.

"I'm sure there are plenty more where these came from, just keep up your defense," Shenroc stated, slapping his friend on the back and ducking under a launched goblin spear.

As goblins died all around them, more came piling into the throne room from adjacent rooms carved into the cave walls. The bodies stacked like firewood as the orcs continued to send the fodder to wear down the defenders. Each time an arrow got through the shield defense, Di'eslo was quick to remove it and heal the wound, and the companions cut down the goblins virtually unscathed.

It did not take long for the mass of goblin attackers to overwhelm the ability of Tiane and Heishi to kill from afar, and the wave made it to melee range, crashing against the shields. Goblins bit, scratched, and swung crude axes and swords at the defenders, causing little damage but beginning to fatigue the shield bearers. With a roar, Shenroc leapt over Di'eslo, his claymore swinging in a wide arc that decapitated two goblins and cut a third in half at the waist. Into the sea of monsters, he waded, eyes bloodshot and foam forming at the edges of his mouth around his tusks as his rage grew. He immediately began taking minor hits from the simple weapons being used against him, but each hit caused him to grow stronger in his bloodlust, his orcish heritage taking control. Di'eslo stepped to the side and focused on keeping a constant stream of healing light on Shenroc, empowering the berserker to charger deeper into the line of attackers.

Yutri, seeing his friend disappearing deeper into the line of monsters, laughed all the harder and pushed forward to follow. Keeping his shield before him, he continued to pick off the makeshift missiles thrown by the soon-to-be-dead attackers as he swung his mighty mithril war hammer like a blacksmith at work. Goblin heads exploded all around him with each swing, as he made a game of knocking them from their feet and into the oncoming attackers. Confusion ran amuck, and the wild giant dwarf reveled in it, laughing and singing as he bathed in the black blood of his enemies.

Deciding he would be more effective in the melee, Heishi recalled his daggers to himself and utilized the power of his ring to add poison to his blade as he ripped it from its saya. He watched Shenroc disappear into the middle of the throng of attackers, only visible by the steady stream of blue light emanating from Di'eslo and reaching out to keep him from falling. Yutri was making his way to the left, pushing back the wave of attackers and singing all the way, the bulk of his height showing above the shorter goblins he dispatched with abandon. Tiane continued to rain death with his bow, occasionally taking down an orc or two who had yet to enter the battle. With a grin, Heishi moved off to the right, slipping in behind a group of goblins attempting to engage the enraged half-orc. With a thought, he ignited the lightning of his blade, the electricity popping and hissing wildly as if the blade itself could feel the coming bloodshed.

In a whirlwind, Heishi ripped into the backs of the goblins rushing toward Shenroc. He was used to having to be more controlled than this when he sparred with martial weapons, but the fight before him was too wild for such tactics. A makeshift spear made of wood with a sharpened point grazed his right cheek as he took the head from a goblin, and he turned to see the last of the goblins pushing toward him and the first orcs entering the fight. He stabbed his blade into the body of a dead goblin beside him, threw all three of his daggers in rapid succession, ripped his blade from the body and continued adding to the carnage before the first dagger struck its target. He focused on the air around him, and felt them moving around him, speeding his every movement. He thrust his blade through the final goblin on his side, then rolled to his left as a monstrous axe just missed his chest. As he came up from the roll, he sliced through the knees of the orc wielding the axe, cutting through both and dropping it to the ground. He ignored that one, opting to let it bleed out as he rushed forward into the remaining orcs rushing him.

In the center of the melee, Shenroc continued to take hits, his blood mixing with that of his enemies, but Di'eslo was quick to close the wounds and keep him in the fight. The final goblins fell as he burst through the line, and he found himself face-to-face with a behemoth of an orc commander. The surprise was evident on both faces that this half-orc had made it this far, but the commander recovered quickly and shoved a barbed spear toward his face. Parrying just in the nick of time with the flat side of his blade, Shenroc shifted his weight to the left as he raised the wicked blade above his right shoulder and brought it down with all his might. The orc was fast enough to get his spear in place to parry the blow, but the wood was not sturdy enough to defend against the kris blade, which ripped through the spear handle as if it was made of paper, cutting cleanly into the shoulder of his opponent. The blade stuck in bone, and Shenroc kicked the commander in the chest, attempting to wrench his blade free, but it was buried too deeply in bone and cartilage. He dodged to the right as the orc slapped him aside, rolling with the blow and drawing his twin daggers as he returned to his feet in a crouch.

The orc stared in disbelief at this puny half-breed before him as he threw the bottom half of his severed spear toward his opponent. Shenroc easily dodged the makeshift weapon, reaching out with his right hand and stabbing the commander in the forearm with his blade, ripping through the crude armor and the flesh of its arm. The commander bellowed in pain, thrusting the top half of the spear in the face of the man who was killing him, but it was no use, Shenroc was simply too fast for him. As he slid under the point of the spear, Shenroc reached up with his left hand and slashed his dagger deep into the right wrist of the commander. Both hands now virtually useless, the orc leaned his head forward in a desperate attempt to rip the throat out of his attacker with his teeth, but once again the smaller half-breed anticipated the attack, retracting his right blade and sliding it smoothly under the chin of the commander, thrusting it upward and burying it in his brain.

The bloodshot eyes of the commander opened wide as he realized he had been killed, then his body went slack as Shenroc removed his daggers, kicking the corpse to the floor and working to free his embedded claymore.

Yutri, still singing and swinging his hammer like a madman, heard a shout from his right and looked over just in time to see the commander fall. With a cheer, he doubled the speed of his attacks, swatting the final goblins around him aside and tearing into the flank of the orc guards. Seeing their commander dispatched so easily by a half-breed, the orcs lost all heart for the fight and retreated in all directions. Attempting to escape along the edges of the cavern, they forgot the only entrance was sealed, and all five of the companions converged on the remaining guards and cut them down as they ran into the closed stone door. The carnage was complete, and not a single orc or goblin remained standing after the slaughter: the reign of King Sgel the Nasty had come to an end.

Chapter 11 – The Orb

"All clear, Top," Tiane stated as he approached Heishi, who was surveying the aftermath of the battle.

"It would appear so. It would seem it is time to see what all the fuss is about," Heishi replied, staring at the orb that remained next to the corpse of Sgel. Tentatively, he walked toward the throne, picking his path around the corpses of goblins and orcs alike.

The remainder of the group converged on the throne, curiously watching as Heishi reached to pick up the mysterious orb, which had turned solid black after falling from the dead hand of Sgel. As he retrieved the fallen orb, a cloud of red smoke encircled him, originating around the orb and creeping out until it made a full circuit around his body, ending once again in the orb, which once again had swirls of red breaking up the solid black of the sphere. His eyes rolled backward in his head so his companions could only see the white of his eyes, and his feet lifted several inches off the floor before depositing him back on the hard surface.

What the companions could not see or

ever understand was the images which flooded his mind as his skin met the mysterious orb. Unseen by the others, images of a massive army of orcs marching toward a castle with a white banner and an indistinguishable emblem emblazoned in the center flashed through his mind. He could see a second army converging on the castle in the distance, and the picture in his mind zoomed in closer and he recognized the second army was made up of the same race of shark-people Jim commanded in Terminus. From a separate direction came an enormous cloud of smoke, with indistinguishable forms moving back and forth inside the dimness. A cloud floated above this mass of moving smoke, darker than the depths of night, and when Heishi looked upon it he felt the chill of death creep through his body. Barely visible on the wall of the castle were defenders in armor that shone like the sun, even in the shadows of the approaching darkness.

Soon the images faded, leaving an impression on his mind but no longer fully taking over his vision. He stood before his companions, his eyes returned to a brighter shade of green than they were previously, feet solidly on the ground once more, and the red swirls of the orb moving less quickly than when he was receiving the vision. Everywhere he looked his vision was sharpened, taking notice of small details previously unseen, and finding himself able to anticipate the movements of his restless companions before they were made. Heishi blinked his eyes a few times, attempting to differentiate between the vision and the real world, then gently set the orb on the rotting throne of Sgel the Nasty, tentatively removing his hand and watching the red swirls slowly dissipate from the face of the orb.

"What just happened, my friend?" Shenroc asked, breaking the tension in the throne room.

"When I touched that thing," Heishi started, nodding his head toward the orb, "I saw something that is difficult to describe. I saw two distinct armies, one of orcs and goblins and one of those shark-men like Jim..."

"Chondri," interrupted Di'eslo.

"Chondri?" asked Heishi, momentarily distracted from his explanation.

"The 'shark-people' from which Big Jim descends are called Chondri. A very dangerous and war-like race. I am honestly surprised he did not storm this place himself to kill everything that lives and retrieve the orb for himself. Chondri desire nothing more in this life than to take the life of others...and then eat them," Di'eslo finished with a wicked grin.

"Fine, I saw an army of orcs and goblins and a second army of Chondri marching toward a castle with a white banner flying above it. The banner had a crest emblazed in the center that I could not make out, but there were what appeared to be men on the walls standing in gleaming armor against the oncoming armies. On a third side, I could see a great cloud of smoke descending with something moving inside of it, and a gigantic cloud floating above it. Then everything faded away and I was back in this room, but my vision has sharpened considerably after returning to 'normal.'"

"I fear one of two outcomes for this vision you received, my friend." Di'eslo stated as the others hung on his every word. "The first possibility is that you have glimpsed future events, which would make sense considering we know an army of orcs were moving in a tunnel above us earlier. I believe the city you witnessed was *Harmonui,* which is an Elvish city by the sea. Tell me, can you remember any details at all of this city?"

"Only that the walls were white and there appeared to be a moat around the outside with a drawbridge. I could not see the rear of the city, only the face of it, so I do not know if there was a sea or not," Heishi replied, straining to remember the vision.

"I do believe that is Harmonui, so I hope this first possibility is correct and that you witnessed a future event. The cloud of smoke descending on the city could very well be my people, which would not bode well for the people of Harmonui if three armies march on them. If this is a future event, there remains time to warn the people of coming danger so they may be prepared," Di'eslo finished, staring vacantly across the room.

"And the second possible outcome of the vision?" Heishi asked, fearing he already knew the answer.

"The second possibility is that you witnessed a current event, and the people of Harmonui are even now being overrun by these three armies. If this city falls, there are not many who will stand against an army the size of which you describe," Di'eslo slowly answered, his gaze still affixed on a spot in the darkness.

"We are faced with several problems at this juncture," Heishi began, causing all eyes to focus on him. "First of all, there is no way I am giving that orb to Jim, especially if an army of Chondri are mobilizing to attack a civilized city." The heads of his companions all bobbed in agreement with that statement. "That leads to the second problem, which is this: why did Jim not come retrieve this orb himself? He had to know I would touch it, so why risk it?"

"I can answer that question, my puny friend," Yutri spoke up, surprising the group. "You have not figured this out yet? And you say *I* am not good with puzzles?" he laughed, staring at Shenroc. "The answer is simple: this room was created in the past by dwarves, as you can see by the craftsmanship of the door, pillars, and walls. It is protected from any who are not already inside, so even we would not have entered unless Sgel decided we were no threat." He glanced at the body of the orc king on the floor beside him. "I guess he was as dumb as he was ugly," he finished, then burst out laughing at his own joke.

"That is a simple explanation which makes sense," Heishi replied, nodding approvingly at the giant dwarf. "In my experience, if there is a simple explanation it usually is the right one, with the exception of explaining how I traveled through a rip in the planes of existence..." A nervous laugh from the group prompted him to continue. "We will assume at this point that Jim has attempted to retrieve the orb himself but was not able to enter the room, so he sent a smaller group to attempt infiltration. He knows my desire to discover the circumstances of my arrival on this plane, and severely underestimated my ability to ignore what I saw," his eyes flashed with a dangerous gleam as he finished speaking.

"We are going to war against Jim, I assume?" Shenroc asked tentatively.

"Terminus is your home. I understand if you

are unwilling to come with me in this, but I am going to kill Jim and attempt to stop the invasion of a peaceful city," Heishi answered with grave sincerity.

"You know I'm always with you, boss," Tiane grinned. "I need to figure out a way to reload ammo here though, I burned through a stack of it hunting before I realized I wouldn't get a resupply around here..."

"Not much chance we will be able to go in guns blazing, my brother. Besides, I foresee a lot of indoor fighting where your rifle will be less effective anyway. We will have to do this the old-fashioned way," Heishi grinned as he reached back to feel the grip of his sword, "and after this work is complete, we will work on finding a way to make gunpowder and reload your rounds." As he stopped speaking, he turned toward the other three, waiting patiently for their answer.

Di'eslo slowly smiled, the shadows curling from his skin as he pondered the thought of destroying Jim. "I am with you, Heishi. You have accepted me as an equal, which is more than I can say for Jim and his lackeys. If my people are marching against Harmonui, I will accompany you in warning my surface cousins to build a strong defense."

Yutri looked at Shenroc, awaiting his answer. "Well, my oldest friend, do we go to war?"

Shenroc slowly nodded his head before answering. "Terminus is my home and has been for most of my life. I was lucky to be allowed a position as a guard, as most would not look past my heritage. However, I have seen how Jim oppresses the people of Terminus, and if there is a chance of freeing them from his tyranny, I say risking my life is a small price to pay. If Yutri is with me, then I will accompany you on this fool's quest."

Having decided upon a course of action, the only remaining loose end was the orb. No one wanted to touch it, and there was reasonable concern that forces of evil would descend on the group the moment it was removed from the protected Dwarven halls.

"Heishi, you may borrow this until a suitable solution is discovered," Di'eslo stated, handing a small pouch to the man before him. "Do not worry, the orb will fit inside easily: it opens to an extra-dimensional portal where the inside of the pouch has more room than the exterior would imply."

"Are you telling me the interior of the pouch is larger than the exterior?" Heishi asked with a grin that only Tiane understood.

"Precisely. Not only will it remove the weight from any object placed inside, but it will completely remove the item from this dimension. If forces of evil are tracking the movement of that orb, it will disappear completely from their sight inside this bag," Di'eslo explained.

Taking the bag from Di'eslo, Heishi cautiously approached the rotten throne, holding the sides of the bag open wide, and scooped the orb into it without allowing any contact between the orb and his hands. As the orb disappeared into the bag, the air in the cavern seemed to lose some of the weight that had been pressing on the companions since entering. It still reeked of rotten meat and hides, and the bodies strewn around the floor added extra odor and filth to the atmosphere, but the air itself no longer felt as heavy, as if a burden had been lifted.

"Well, that, as they say, is that," Heishi stated, tying the bag to his belt.

"Who says this?" Yutri asked, looking confused.

"Never mind, it is a saying in my world. Come, my friends, let us search this cavern for anything of use, and then return to pay Jim a visit," Heishi smiled.

After deciding to search the throne room starting in the rear and working toward the magical door, the companions began their search. Smaller rooms had been cut into the walls, creating sleeping areas, kitchens, and even a forge room by some ancient inhabitant of the cavern. The hieroglyphics on the walls confirmed what Yutri had assumed, Dwarves had built this hall centuries past, although there were no answers as to what happened to them or why this single cavern was the only room worked into the rough caves above.

Unfortunately, the orc inhabitants had left nothing of value to the group. There remained plenty of rotten food and moldy bread, rusty weapons and mismatched pieces of roughly made armor, but nothing worth plundering. They had worked their way on opposite walls about halfway through the cavern, roughly even with the throne in the center of the room, when Shenroc let out a sharp call to rally the companions. As he approached, Heishi saw the half-orc was feverishly working to break the lock on a cage that was mounted into the wall of the room he had been searching. Before he could inquire as to the reason for the call, he then saw a dirty, naked elf female locked in the cage, breathing heavily and barely conscious.

As the lock sprung, Yutri was there to gently remove the elf from the cage, wrapping her in his traveling cloak to retain as much of her modesty as was possible. Di'eslo pointed to a table in the room, and Yutri placed the elf on the table with as much care as a mother laying down her child. The elf's eyes fluttered upon being stretched out on the table, but otherwise did not respond.

"Stay close, my large friend," Di'eslo whispered to Yutri, "when the healing enters her, she may awaken, and we do not know what her state of mind will be. I have no doubt she has been abused by these monsters," he cast an apologetic glance at Shenroc when he realized what he had said, who shrugged as if to admit to the brutal nature of the orc race. He then held out his shield to help focus, and a steady stream of blue light came from the spider web design and entered the elf, causing the cuts to close themselves, bones to knit back together, and bruises to disappear before the eyes of the companions.

After a few minutes of working to heal the young female, Di'eslo lowered his shield and stepped back as she opened her eyes slowly. Seeing a shadow elf and a half-orc beside her, she began to leap to her feet, but was stopped by the giant dwarf standing beside her.

"Easy, girl, easy, he is a friend. He just healed you from whatever the orcs did to you," Yutri explained in a soft voice as he held her as carefully as possible. He looked at Shenroc, realized how he appeared to her covered in orc and goblin blood, and laughed softly. "That one is also a friend, although he does not appear to be so. He has saved my life many times and is even now covered in the blood of your captors. Be safe, little elf, no one here will harm you."

Heishi stepped between Di'eslo and his patient, hoping to block her view of her dark cousin. "Lady, may we inquire your name and how you came to be here?"

The elf looked around at the strange group of companions surrounding her before shakily answering, "My name is Gabrielle Anaoilin, and you will receive no ransom for me, if that is what you expect, human." She glared at Heishi defiantly, and although she clearly was still recovering from her captivity, a fire burned in her crystal blue eyes.

"Ma'am, I do not want a ransom for you. I do not even know who you are. My companions and I were deceived into coming down here to retrieve something for Big Jim in Terminus..." Heishi began but stopped suddenly due to the look that crossed her face when he mentioned Jim. "Do you know Jim?"

"That monster is who ordered the attack on my ship. His minions captured me at sea and dragged me back to that city. He traded me to these orcs for some crystal ball, and I later overheard the orc king laughing about tricking Jim with a worthless bauble and gaining a valuable prisoner. Apparently, he knew nothing of preserving his merchandise, as they beat me repeatedly. I have lost all track of time in here and know not whether a ransom demand was sent to my family in Harmonui or not," the elf stated with a venomous look on her face.

"Have no fear, lady, you are safe with us. After killing Sgel the Nasty, we came to understand that we had been used by Jim and have just recently decided we will kill him. This must be fate, as we were then going to Harmonui to warn of an imminent attack by three armies. We will see you safely home, lady," Heishi said as warmly as possible, attempting to calm the erratic elf.

She paused to consider his proposal, began to nod, then noticed she was naked, save the giant cloak wrapped loosely around her body. A look of outrage crossed her face as she slapped Heishi across the face. "Do. You. Know. Who. I. AM?" she asked, pausing to pronounce every syllable of every word as it exited her mouth.

"No, ma'am, I do not. We also are not the ones who removed your clothing, so if anything, you should be thanking my associate Yutri for covering you with his cloak. We will search for more appropriate clothing for you, but in the meantime, we would appreciate if you stopped hitting us since we saved you from your cage," Heishi replied while controlling his desire to slap her back.

"That is fair human and thank you for releasing me. I am still adjusting to my freedom, and do not mean to disrespect you or your companions," she paused, looking at Di'eslo, "except maybe for *him.*"

"He is the one who healed your wounds. *He* has kept everyone before you alive for the past days. *He* deserves your gratitude, not your disdain because of the color of his skin, *lady,"* Heishi replied, then stomped away, asking the others in the team to search for some clothing for the elf.

Having found a loose-fitting robe and some soft leather boots, presumably stolen from traveling merchants, in another of the rooms adjacent to the throne room, Gabrielle was dressed and able to walk tentatively around. Di'eslo approached her as she searched for her belongings in a pile of gear strewn about the room, and when she noticed him her back stiffened as she turned to face the shadow elf.

"M'lady, I have rested sufficiently to allow me to further heal your wounds. I noticed you are still having difficulty walking and can assist with that if you will allow me," he said, politely bowing slightly as he finished speaking.

"Yes, that would be lovely, and thank you, Di'eslo. I should not have spoken to you as I did, but I am sure you were taught all surface elves are evil when you were young, and the same prejudices follow my perception of you."

"There is no need to apologize, lady," Di'eslo stated as he began to focus on the healing wave he was sending toward her. "Your perceptions of my people are founded, where I have found that mine of your people are not. In my time on the surface, I have come to understand and expect such reactions, and believe me, no offense was taken."

As the healing waves entered her body, rejuvenating her and knitting torn muscles and bone together, Gabrielle smiled at the mysterious shadow elf, enjoying his company and gracious answer.

Chapter 12 – The Beginning of the End

Having found nothing of use in the cave, the companions, now six strong, began making their way back to the surface. Exiting the throne room proved a simple task, as the door slid open easily from the inside, and Heishi decided to leave it open for the subterranean rats and other carrion eaters to clean up the mess. Having left virtually invisible marks on their way down into the tunnels, Shenroc easily lead them to the cave on the surface in a fraction of the time it took to work their way to the bottom. The bodies of the dead goblins had already been dragged away by something, and other than a few dark stains on the stone floor no one would ever know what had taken place here.

The group paused to eat a fast meal in the cave, reveling in the sunlight spilling through the opening, then began to backtrack to Terminus following the map Heishi held. As they walked, Heishi brought Gabrielle up to speed on everything that happened to him in the recent days while never forgetting to keep tight security, remembering the ekastatu attack. He described the shift in planes, his experience in

Terminus, the encounter with Jim, and their quest to find the orb. When describing the vision he received when he touched the orb, he was a bit guarded in the description, focusing mainly on the three armies converging on a city Di'eslo assumed was Harmonui. He left out the current location of the orb, innocently disguised in the bag attached to his belt, and she did not press the issue.

The return to Terminus proved uneventful, with only a single instance where the companions hid on the side of the road as a caravan rolled past: there was no need to announce their presence before they arrived. As they turned onto the road to the front gate, Di'eslo once again donned his gloves and cloak, pulling the hood up to cover his face from unwanted attention. The sun was setting as they finally reached the gate and were able to slip through unmolested as the guards began locking down the city for the night.

Heading for the docks, the companions decided upon finding a room at an inn for the night so they could have a meal and get rest before the confrontation with Jim. Shenroc lead the group to an inn several blocks from The Portal, where the food was adequate and the rooms were less comfortable, but anonymity was more likely. They ate their meal in silence, not wanting any conversation to be overheard by the drunk patrons of the establishment, then retired to upstairs rooms. Later in the night, they met in the room shared by Shenroc and Yutri to discuss the strategy for the morning.

"We need to secure passage to Harmonui before our confrontation with Jim and his goons. If it goes well, we will need to leave in a hurry with no questions asked," Heishi began the conversation.

"I can help with that, Yutri and I have contacts on the docks, we will find the first ship leaving tomorrow. The worst that might happen is we may have to go to a port out of our way and wait for a ship bound for Harmonui, but it will be in our best interest to leave immediately after you confront Jim," Shenroc replied.

"A solid plan. We still have access to my new blacksmith shop if you need to throw in some armor or weapons to pay for passage on the ship. Is there anything else you may need from us to assist, or should we stay in hiding until you have secured the trip for us?"

Shenroc grinned at his new friend, "Just wait here, human, and stay out of sight. If Jim or any of his spies see you too soon, it will force the confrontation and you may be stuck in a city of his lackeys with no way out. Be patient and let the oaf and me take care of the escape."

Early the next morning, Shenroc and

Yutri wandered to the dock in search of the first ship leaving that morning. As they walked, the two laughed and joked with each other, purposely seeming to be meandering aimlessly down the road, while secretly they were headed straight for the slip of Tylo the Blue, hoping the rotten pirate was in port. If anyone would agree to whisk the companions away from Terminus without alerting the "authorities," it was Tylo.

Turning the corner, they could see the low, sleek ship belonging to Tylo the Blue in his normal slip. The sails were down, and from a distance it appeared the crew was fast at work repairing damage from whatever trouble they had found on their most recent voyage. When the first crew member recognized the pair sauntering up the dock, he called out the approaching visitors to Tylo, who immediately slid down the closest rope to the dock. grabbing Yutri in a massive bear hug. The two stood eye-to-eye, however Tylo was no dwarf, he was of Chondri descent, although he lacked the bulk of Jim and his guards. Tylo was tall, but his body consisted of lean muscle, every bit of his body honed to work in perfect harmony with not a movement wasted. One look at this dangerous predator was enough for most people to steer clear: but Yutri and Shenroc were not normal people.

"Ere now, what're you doin' slummin it

on me dock, ye overgrown son of a gnome?" Tylo asked as he released Yutri from his embrace and reached to snatch Shenroc up.

"Neither of my parents were gnomes, I have told you this repeatedly," Yutri answered, looking a bit confused.

"Never mind all of that," Shenroc interjected before Yutri could get off on a tangent. "We need to seek passage on a fast ship that will be leaving this morning and will not ask questions. I could not find a fast ship, so we decided to see if you were available instead, you old pirate," he finished, barely containing the grin spreading across his face.

"Eh? What's that? You want me to slit your throat and feed you to the fish?" replied a smiling Tylo. "I have also told you repeatedly that I am not a pirate: I am a gentleman adventurer," he stated, giving his best impression of the smooth baritone voice of Yutri.

"You said he was a pirate, Shenroc," a confused Yutri said, turning his head side to side between his two friends.

"To move along the conversation, we will agree upon 'gentleman adventurer,'" Shenroc said, turning to Yutri and mouthing *"which is another name for a pirate,"* which finally brought a smile of understanding from the slow dwarf. "Is your fine vessel available for a leisurely cruise out of this harbor to pretty much anywhere in the world that is not here?"

Staring at Yutri, Tylo muttered, "Sure be good for ye that ye are a devil in a fight, er someone woulda killed ye dead by now." Turning his head toward Shenroc, he began to nod slowly, "Aye, me friend, I kin be available to take ye on a, ahh, pleasure cruise on short notice this fine mornin' if ye be needin' it. I will be needin' to know who ye're takin' along and who need not know about yer trip..."

Shenroc locked stares with his pirate friend, contemplating how much he should divulge. Finally, he tentatively stated in a low voice, "Big Jim will not see the light of another day. I have two humans, a shadow elf, and a high elf who need to be delivered out of this harbor with all haste after the deed is done. Their destination is Harmonui, but the main objective is to leave Terminus while still breathing; wherever you can take them would be appreciated."

Nodding his head in understanding, Tylo glared at Shenroc as he asked, "I don't suppose ye have a payment fer this trip, do ye?"

With a sigh of relief and a sly grin, Tylo tosses the pirate a set of keys. "Do you remember Orra? She used to be a decent blacksmith before she tried to eat my human friend. Those are the keys to her shop, anything in it now belongs to Tylo the Blue."

Tylo paused for a moment, staring at the keys in his hand, then nodded. "Aye, this be payment enough, what be the sign that we be needin' to leave?"

"I would make ready now and leave an eye out toward the Portal. If I know my new companions at all, it will be obvious when we are ready to depart…"

A short time later, the two returned to the inn where the remainder of the companions were just finishing their morning meal. Heishi looked up as Shenroc approached and seeing the pleased look on the half-orc's face, he nodded. "We are all set for this morning then, my friend?"

"Aye, we are. I have booked us passage on a cruise ship with a 'gentleman adventurer.' who is preparing to depart as we speak. The passage to Harmonui is paid in full, my associate accepted the keys to your blacksmith shop as payment," Shenroc explained.

"Good, I do not plan on coming back here to run a business, and we already took everything we need from the shop. Now, explain to me what a 'gentleman adventurer' is in this world. I am not picky about our avenue of departure but need to know more about who is taking us, so I know whether or not we need to secure different transportation once we are safely away from Terminus," Heishi replied.

"Tylo the Blue refers to himself as a 'gentleman adventurer' because he dislikes being called a pirate. I see the look you are giving me, my friend, but do not be so hasty in your judgment of him. Pirate is a very broad term, and in the broadest sense yes, he is a pirate in that he attacks other ships, loots them, and typically kills all aboard before sinking the ship to cover his involvement in the disappearance of the ship. However, he is not a cutthroat with no heart: he does not attack innocent vessels. Tylo prefers to think of himself as an equalizer: he attacks trade ships flying the flag of a corrupt city, such as Terminus, knowing that all aboard are thieves and murderers themselves, whether sanctioned by the government of their city or not. He does not kill women, children, or those who have been forced into service by a tyrant: those he gives free passage to the closest port, assuming they agree to remain silent as to who was responsible for the disappearance of their ship. Is this a man you can do business with?"

After a few moments of contemplation, Heishi nodded before answering, "Yes, my friend, I can respect a man who targets tyrannical governments. There is a saying in my world, 'the only difference between a terrorist and a freedom fighter is whether or not you win.' I think the same applies to your pirate friend."

"Yes, I like this saying. You should teach this to Tylo when you meet him, I believe he will appreciate the name 'freedom fighter.'"

As the two talked, Gabrielle approached the table, waiting patiently for a chance to interrupt the conversation. The two turned to her, and she began a bit hesitantly, "I just wanted to say thank you for saving me and being patient with me. I have never met an orc," she said, looking at Shenroc, "who did not want to kill me. Same goes for a shadow elf," she glanced to the adjacent table where Di'eslo was finishing his meal under the cover of his hood. "I do appreciate everything, and when I am returned to Harmonui, I will repay you for your kindness. Until that time, please just know that I am grateful and will do anything I can to assist you in your, umm, activities today." She finished with a slight pink shade coloring her beautiful cheeks and the tips of her ears.

"Well, my lady, I can honestly say I have never in my life made an elf blush, so I suppose that is payment enough for you reacting to my presence with caution," Shenroc said with mock gravity. "Consider all past transgressions forgiven, and may we move forward in friendship."

The elf smiled and bobbed her head in agreement.

Tiane leaned forward as the two stared weirdly at each other, breaking the silence. "Now that everyone is one big happy family, what is the plan here, Top? We could just jump on this pirate ship and leave, no questions asked, and this Jim character would never find us. Do we really need to risk our lives this late in the game just because he pissed you off?"

The question was posed in a louder tone than intended, but luckily the room was empty except for the companions and the bartender, who was well versed in not hearing conversations in his bar. Each of the companions leaned closer to Heishi to hear his response to the question most had been thinking but only Tiane had the nerve to ask.

"That is a fair question, my brother. I believe my path is clear before me, I need to do this. I will not think any less of any man, or woman, who feels like this is a fool's errand and would rather go wait on the ship. To answer your question, this is not simply because Jim 'pissed me off,' and not because he tried to use me for his own designs because I did not know what he was asking me to do. I look around this town and I see a city under the shadow of a dictator. I see good people who are oppressed by a tyrant. You served with me in both Iraq and Afghanistan, Staff Sergeant Tiane: were we there for oil? Were we there to protect a drug trade? No! You know better. We were there to help the people of those countries because they were being oppressed by insurgent terrorists.

"That is how I see Terminus. We can either leave on this pirate ship and never look back at the pain and suffering of the people who live here, or we can make a difference. I choose to make a difference and remove this dictator from power, allowing the people here to get ahead in their lives. Will it help? Maybe. But we must try, and personally I would rather die here helping people than out on a pirate ship, so the reward more than justifies the risk. Do what you will, but my path leads to The Portal this morning to end this."

As he spoke, one at a time the members of the party who had been questioning their decision to attack Jim moment ago all looked down in embarrassment. Silence hung like a wet blanket over the group, each one struggling with the thought of a suicide mission but not wanting to walk away from the people of Terminus.

Tiane broke the silence first. "Top, you know I was going to follow you anyway. I didn't mean to ever sound disloyal; I was just asking a question. You always had me with you, but now I want to go to help, not just because I will follow you anywhere."

Heishi nodded his approval as he clapped his hand on the shoulder of the young sniper.

"I owe you my life. Do not take that for granted, human. I would follow you until I repay that debt anyway, but I also owe Jim a debt of a different sort. I will not leave Terminus with that overgrown minnow still drawing breath," Gabrielle finished with a wicked grin.

One by one, every member of the party acknowledged their willingness to walk into certain death either to be with Heishi or to repay Jim for one wrong or another done to them. As the conversation continued, it became obvious the bartender was having a difficult time ignoring them, and he crept closer and closer to the group, listening to their plans.

Jumping to his feet and smashing a table to pieces with his mithril war hammer, Yutri stared the bartender directly in the eye as he addressed the small man: "Do you hear something of interest to you?"

"Oh, no, sir, what you and your companions discuss is of no concern to me! I was simply straightening up and cleaning the tables while I wait for the morning crowd," the nervous bartended stuttered.

Waiving the bartender away, Yutri returned to the table as Shenroc explained, "That was a clear warning to us: there will soon be a crowd of people coming to break their fast. We need to be gone from this place before that happens, because if he does not report our discussion, he will be held accountable to Jim should we fail. I do not fault the little weasel for this, it is just what he must do if he wants to continue living in Terminus."

"That settles it then," Heishi began. "I think our path is clear before us: it's time to make the green grass grow."

Chapter 13 – The End and the Beginning

The sun was up, and the streets were stirring with morning business when the companions exited the inn, tossing a few extra gold pieces to the bartender with the unspoken threat to keep his mouth shut until they were well away. Abandoning all pretenses of a peaceful stroll down the street, the group picked up a wedge formation with Yutri leading, parting the crowd before them, and Di'eslo protected in the rear where he could focus on keeping them alive. After the first block, pedestrians began parting well in advance of the approaching group, armed for battle and faces set in the direction of The Portal.

Yutri, being in the lead, was the first to reach the front door of the bar, which he subsequently kicked off its hinges and sent flying across the room. The companions slid into a single file as they cleared the door jam, then spread back out into the bar: Heishi and Tiane to his right, Shenroc and Gabrielle to his left, with Di'eslo in the center of the formation, weapons out and facing into the room for any danger.

The little bartender, seeing them burst through the door, let out a yelp and went scurrying toward the door to the office occupied by Jim, bumping into every table and chair along the way as his eyes spun about crazily in his head. As he ran, Heishi had a moment of compassion, desiring to let this miserable wretch live. He thought better as he remembered the bartender laughing as he set Heishi up to fight a hungry Chondri, and he whipped all three daggers across the room in rapid succession, burying them between his shoulder blades and sending the whelp bouncing against the door.

"That's one for me, try to keep up young Staff Sergeant," Heishi said with a grin.

"Doesn't count, Top, that one was running away, and my granny would have hit him from here," Tiane replied, smoothly pulling an arrow from his quiver, knocking it, and letting it fly into the face of the first Chondri who opened a side door to enter the room. "That one, however, does count."

"Petty humans, you will never beat me at this game, or in love," Yutri stated as he let out a full belly laugh and rushed toward the door where the first Chondri guard had fallen.

Before he made it across the room, four more guards piled through the door and into the room. Tiane was able to put an arrow into the shoulder of the first one, who move surprisingly quickly for someone so big, but then Yutri was amid them and more arrows flying would endanger his friends. He slung the bow on his back, jerked his kamas from their holsters, activating the blades and flames with a thought, and rushed in behind the giant dwarf.

A hidden door on the right side of the room opened, with six more gigantic Chondri guards spilling through it into the room, and before the melee could be joined with these six, five more entered through the front door behind the companions.

Whipping his claymore around toward the front door, Shenroc roared in blissful rage as he rushed the newcomers. "Now THIS is my idea of a fair fight!" he bellowed, severing the sword arm from his first opponent before he had time to realize the orc was coming towards him headfirst. The half-orc swung with abandon, taking small hits in exchange for huge swings of his claymore, removing body parts from his opponents with each swing. As he rushed the door, more of the Chondri piled in from somewhere on the street, replacing each fallen opponent with two more.

Behind Shenroc, Heishi turned toward the six guards who entered through the previously hidden door, recalling his daggers to himself and letting them fly toward the latest attackers.

He scored no fatal hits with the projectiles, but they slowed his opponents as he focused on the air currents to speed himself up. His sword blazed with emerald electrical currents that flared with his focus, leaping from the blade to enter his victims before his blade even made contact. His entire body became a weapon, sliding past blades aimed to decapitate him, landing an elbow to the face of an attacker here, a knee to the groin there, and always following through with a swipe of his deadly sword that left at least one piece of the Chondri on the floor.

To the other side, Yutri was singing again, this time a tawdry song more appropriate for a brothel than anywhere else, but he was effectively pushing his opponents back against the wall, and with nowhere to run he was crushing bone with each swing of his war hammer. Tiane worked around his large companion, putting his flaming kamas to work. The hammer would swing high, and a kama would follow low at the same time, crushing bone and slicing through flesh simultaneously. The two quickly found a symbiotic rhythm, and within moments all four had been prepared for an undertaker; however, more guards continued through the door, pressing the two back a few steps to regroup before pushing forward again.

Di'eslo was kept busy through this simply keeping the companions alive. He thoroughly enjoyed putting his flail to work when the opportunity arose, but these companions of his were reckless, attacking with abandon and assuming he would keep them from meeting their maker. *So be it,* Di'eslo thought as he kept a steady stream of healing light poured on the wild Shenroc, *if Jim falls because I kept these maniacs alive, it is almost as satisfying as if I split his skull myself.* Pulling his cloak from his face to better focus on his companions, he saw a few of the Chondri take a step back in surprise. His companions, no novices to battle, did not miss a beat and cut them down while they were distracted.

It was beginning to appear the fight would be won with no trouble when the rear door burst open and Big Jim stepped through, hurling lifeless corpse of the bartender across the room and into Yutri like a missile. Yutri never missed a beat as the body crashed into his side, swiping it away and finishing off the last of the guards on his side. Yutri and Tiane turned toward Big Jim when their sector was cleared, ready to fend off any attacks from the massive Chondri. Likewise, Shenroc was just clearing the doorway, hacking guards to pieces and leaving them to writhe in agony as he finished off the rest in his way. He kicked his last opponent in the face on the ground and whipped around to face Jim, the whites of his eyes not visible through the red, and his mouth covered in foam around his tusks where he had whipped himself into a frenzy. Heishi finished off his opponents with style, the lightning flashing as he removed the head from his final opponent and turned to face Jim.

"What do you think you are doing, you ungrateful wretches?" bellowed Jim as he donned his helmet and ripped his massive sword from its scabbard, his armor casting blood colored reflections around the room in the light from the missing front door and the fireplace on the wall where Yutri had launched a dead guard who was now aflame. "I allowed each of you to live and work in MY city, I even offered to pay you to return my orb, and you come in my bar like THIS? Killing my men?"

Heishi stalked across the room, never taking his eyes from Jim, and stopped just out of range of the massive sword the Chondri boss had pointed his direction. "I suppose selling this elf maiden was just business. And sending me to my death, I should *thank* you? You knew what was down in those caves. You knew how powerful the orb made Sgel the Nasty. You forced my companions to go to their deaths, while tricking me into unwittingly going.

But that is not the worst of it, Jim. You are being held accountable for your treatment of the people of Terminus. That is right, you little tyrant, we are relieving you of your hold on this city and giving it to the people. No longer will they live in fear of you and your thugs. No longer will they eat scraps while you live in opulence. Normally I would give you the option to turn around and walk away with your head attached," the lightning on the blade of his sword flared as he spoke, "but not today. Today, I am going to do what is best for people everywhere: I am going to remove your head and kick it down the street as the vendors set up for the day."

As he ended, Jim attempted to take advantage of his monologuing, shifting his weight forward and taking a swing with his sword, the light glinting off the blood red edge of the blade as it arced toward Heishi. Far from being caught off guard, Heishi slid back a pace as the sword moved, but was startled when a blue light flashed over his shoulder, smashing into the sword arm swinging it. When the light connected with the sword, ice began to form around his arm and sword, startling Jim as well as his opponents. Heishi risked a glance over his shoulder and saw the source of the light: Gabrielle stood with her palm open and facing Jim, the last fragments of the ice leaving her palm and flying toward the behemoth before her.

She saw Heishi glance her way in

confusion, shrugged a bit, and stated, "What can I say? I like ice…"

Roaring in frustration, Jim jerked his arm away from the ice forming on his armor, crushing it and sending flurries of snow around the room. He used the confusion to bring his massive shield between him and his attackers, the ruby eyes of the shark god glowing a brilliant shade of crimson, and a line of fire spat back at Gabrielle, melting the remnants of ice and super heating it to create steam. As the companions rocked back on their heels to avoid being burned by the steam, Jim swiped to his left with the shield, the golden shark teeth flashing in the light as they ripped through the chain mail, leather, and into the flesh of Heishi's left arm, severing muscle and leaving it hanging limp at his side as he rolled to the right to avoid the attack.

Yutri leapt into action to defend his new friend, thrusting his shield forward to block the sword which swung back toward Heishi to decapitate him. He successfully blocked the attack, but mis-judged the power behind the swing, which connected with his shield and left his arm a bit numb as he attempted a counter swing with his mithril hammer. The swing connected, and although he was fully balanced and put all his considerable power into the attack, it thudded against the plate armor covering Jim's chest and did nothing more than slide him backward a pace or two in the blood and guts covering the floor. A look of shock spread across his face as Jim grinned, rows of sharp teeth glistening, and the golden teeth of the shield slid back across and connected squarely with the shield Yutri presented, sending him flying back across the room and smashing into Heishi.

Di'eslo slid behind the fighters, focusing on the spider web on his shield, and releasing the stored energy within the web. A large purple web flew across the room, glowing with unrestrained power, and wrapped around Jim's sword arm, immobilizing it against his body. He then turned his attention to Heishi, who was bleeding out from his limp left arm as he struggled to detangle himself from Yutri and gain his footing again. The healing wave reached out toward the man, and the muscle and tissue began to knit back together as he charged back into the fight.

Shenroc, seeing his oldest friend tossed to the side like a toy, bellowed in rage, rushing forward with his claymore swinging in a figure eight motion, swatting aside the deadly shield and connecting with the crimson armor behind. His first blow did nothing more than make a loud screeching sound as it connected with the armor and was turned away, but he reached the blade back and aimed for the joint in the armor over Jim's left elbow, and was pleased when the kris blade bit into the joint and slashed through bone and tissue, coming just short of severing the arm completely. As the triumph showed in his eyes and he slid his blade over his head to finish off his opponent, Jim head butted him in the face, flattening his nose as it broke, splattering blood across his face and knocking him from his feet.

As Shenroc fell to the side, a trio of arrows fired in rapid succession flew from the back of the room where Tiane had taken up a position on top of a table where he could get an angle without hitting his companions. The first two arrows bounced harmlessly off the plate armor, but the third buried itself in Jim's right shoulder as he ripped his sword arm loose of the web Di'eslo had entangled him in with a roar of defiance. Jim looked back at Tiane with disdain as his eyes rolled back in his head, showing only a dull black protective covering over them. He swung what remained of his left arm holding his shield toward Tiane and loosed a blast of fire from the ruby eyes of his shark god, ripping through the end of the room and catching it on fire. Tiane deftly rolled to the side, avoiding the blast and keeping up a stream of arrows flying toward the wild Chondri who was wreaking havoc on his friends.

Gabrielle let loose another blast of ice toward the monster, who deflected it with his shield by wildly swinging his limp arm as the blast of fire from the shark god eyes continued flashing around the room. The ice melted and turned to steam, causing Di'eslo to duck behind his shield and pause the healing energy he was directing toward Heishi just as the fire bolt struck his shield and shoved him backward as well.

Jim maintained the constant blast of fire emanating from his shield as he swung his arm wildly in every direction. He screamed in defiance as he set fire to his own bar, the blood and sweat flowing as he desperately glanced around for an exit. As the fire crept up to the second floor, the front wall appeared to be weakening so he rushed toward it to crash through and escape into the street.

Heishi, having recovered enough to stand, rushed toward the dictator, the green electricity of his blade flashing out in direct proportion to his anger. As Jim put his head down and pushed past Yutri like a football linebacker, Heishi spun and brought his blade down in a flashing arc, connecting with the back of Jim's neck and decapitating his hated enemy. The fire bolt from the shield ceased immediately as his head rolled from his shoulders and his body crashed into the floor.

The companions paused for a moment, watching the head roll across the floor and listening to the sound of the walls and ceiling burning. Di'eslo kept the stream of healing coming, alternating between members of the group to relieve each of their pain as quickly as possible. The rest stared at each other, unable to comprehend that they had lived through the battle. Without a word, Heishi walked over to the severed head, picked it up, and walked toward the shattered front door. As he stepped into the street, he noticed a crowd had already gathered to see what was happening. Heishi lifted the severed head with both hands as high as he could reach, and as the onlookers realized what he was holding, he threw it into the street, rolling toward the vendors selling their wares.

Without a word, the companions headed toward the dock to meet with Tylo and escape this place. The fires inside The Portal continued to burn, and all activity on the street came to a halt as the citizens of Terminus watched it burn.

Standing on the dock in front of the *Slip Away*, the ship belonging to Tylo the Blue, Shenroc stopped and grasped Heishi's hand. "My friend, this is where Yutri and I say goodbye. This was a difficult decision for us, but Terminus is our home and we need to stay here and help rebuild. There will be a power vacuum left in the wake of removing Jim from power, and if no one guides the power shift the people here could be left with a tyrant who is worse than Jim ever was. Please understand that we owe you a debt of gratitude we can never repay and would do anything to assist you in the rest of your quest, but we have an obligation to our people here."

Nodding as he listened, Heishi found he was fighting back tears for the first time he could remember in his adult life. "My friend, I could not have survived more than a day in this place if it was not for you. I understand why you must stay and hope that you will find me again when this place is safe for good people to live."

The companions said their goodbyes, then Shenroc and Yutri stepped back and watched the other four board the ship. Tylo saluted the pair from the bow of the ship as it slid away from the dock, then returned to his duties as captain of the vessel.

"Will we see them again?" Yutri asked, not even attempting to hide the tears in his eyes.

"If they live long enough we will," replied Shenroc, then the two turned and walked back to face the ramifications of their actions that morning.

Epilogue

The fire started in The Portal spread beautifully to the surrounding buildings. From each direction, men and women of every race imaginable ran back and forth with buckets of water, attempting to control the blaze. Standing in the stern of the ship as it pulled out of the harbor, Heishi stared at the growing flames and knew it was no use: at least half the city would be ravaged by the fire.

Serves them right. If ever I have seen a city that needed a good purging, it was Terminus. Maybe they will have a chance for a fresh start now. There were good people in Terminus, but they never had a chance under that tyrant Big Jim. I'll have to come back some day and check in on them, and if they haven't learned their lesson, we'll burn it down again. Too easy.

He turned and wandered to the bow, lost in thought. Tiane walked over and stood by his side, looking to the horizon as the sun began to slip into the sea. For a time, they stood quietly, watching the sunset, then Tiane broke the silence:

"So, Heishi, do you think we'll ever find

the rest of the team?"

The silence was deafening as he waited for a response, but Heishi finally looked back and grinned. "I do believe we will. We both counted three other parachutes, so we know the guys potentially survived the jump. From the light in Zatus' eyes, I have to assume he is here somewhere and understands more than we think he does about what is going on. The first thing on the agenda is to make it safely to Harmonui and warn them of the attack. Hopefully somewhere along the way we will pick up some information of other-worlders appearing so we can track them down. Be patient, my brother, you were here for over three months before I arrived, and that has been less than a week. As much as I hate leaving Terminus and the thought of Aki and Zatus arriving there without us, I trust Shenroc and Yutri to keep an eye open for them, and we must deliver this message to the elves. I have never believed in fate, but it would seem we have arrived in this place just in time to assist the forces of good against an encroaching evil, and it is something I feel I have to do."

Tiane nodded and turned back to the horizon as the last rays of sunlight disappeared and his vision shifted into the low light spectrum. He hoped the crew had just been trying to scare the newcomer with their stories of sea monsters, but after everything he had witnessed in this place, he had to assume there was truth to them. He was not afraid, he had nothing to lose at this point, but he kept a watchful eye as the harbor disappeared behind him.

Unseen by those making a hasty getaway on the ship was a dark shape floating effortlessly above the burning city. The shadow dragon glided in circles, occasionally catching an updraft to maintain its elevation. Yellow eyes glinted through the mass of shadows swirling around the beast, obscuring its bulk from the vision of those below as the sky darkened. It watched as the puny beings scampered back and forth, the size of ants from this height, the futility of their efforts making them more pathetic in the eyes of the ancient one.

Its rider, Fion, also cloaked in shadow, looked on with an amused expression. This was a shadow elf in the truest sense of his race: cruel, brutal, and thoroughly evil. Unbeknownst to those escaping the burning city, he was the true power behind Big Jim, the bumbling oaf who had recently perished. Fion shook his head and laughed mercilessly.

"Yes, Dracorex, Jim was a buffoon and received what he deserved. He should know better than to antagonize men of such power.

The Orb is lost to us for now; I do not sense its presence on the puny vessel." Fion sighed and stared at the ship as it disappeared from the harbor.

"Master let me kill them and search the corpses," Dracorex grumbled, his voice sounding like the rumble of distant thunder to those below. It disgusted the Dragon King to call this elf "master," and to feign subservience, but it served his purposes to bring about the destruction to come. A wicked smile crossed the lips of the dragon, razor sharp teeth showing as he thought of destroying the elves and then moving on to the cities of men.

"No, my friend, we must allow them to live until the location of the Orb can be discovered. Then we will send someone to recover it for us. It is too soon to reveal our presence, so bide your time, and soon we will revel in the annihilation that awaits this world."

In the distance along the edge of the mountain, unnoticed by all, a cloud formed, spewing red lightning…

About the Author

Jeff Sabean is married to the love of his life and is the proud father of five wonderful children (and included this to see if they continued to read this far) in Southwest Florida.

He is a Veteran of the US Army, having served multiple combat deployments in both Iraq and Afghanistan with the 82nd Airborne Division, US Army Special Operations Command, and the 25th Infantry Division (Light) between 2004 and 2010. He is also a Second-Degree Black Belt (Nidan) in Shito-Ryu Karate, with a First-Degree Black Belt in Tonfa in Okinawan Kobudo, and has always loved learning Iaido, the art of drawing Japanese swords.

In his free time, Jeff spends most of his time fishing, reading, playing video games, and trying to convince his kids that D&D is cool so they should play with him. He is an avid reader of Epic Fantasy as well as Sci Fi and martial arts books.

Thank you for reading Book 1 of my new Shifting Planes Series! If you enjoyed reading it, please leave feedback to recommend it for others. If you have recommendations for making future stories better, I welcome the critiques, as I am doing this to tell great stories, not just to sell books.

If you would like to keep updated on upcoming releases, please follow me on Facebook and/or join my Official Mailing List. I will periodically send out free sneak peeks at upcoming books, as well as discounts for pre-ordering new titles before they are released!

https://jeffsabean.com

Shifting Planes Series:

Heishi

Aki

Fion (Coming Fall 2019)